Ghost Hunters Adventure Club
AND THE SECRET OF THE
GRANDE CHATEAU

Ghost Hunters Adventure Club
AND THE SECRET OF THE
GRANDE CHATEAU

DR. CECIL H.H. MILLS

PERMUTED
PRESS

A PERMUTED PRESS BOOK

Ghost Hunters Adventure Club and the Secret of the Grande Chateau
© 2020 by Game Grumps
All Rights Reserved

ISBN: 978-1-68261-892-9
ISBN (eBook): 978-1-68261-893-6

Cover illustration by Paul Mann
Cover typography by Cody Corcoran
Back cover photo by Tucker Prescott
Illustrations by Rachel L. Allen
Interior design and composition, Greg Johnson, Textbook Perfect

This book is a work of fiction. People, places, events, and situations are the product of the author's imagination. Any resemblance to actual persons, living or dead, or historical events, is purely coincidental.

PERMUTED
PRESS

Permuted Press, LLC
New York • Nashville
permutedpress.com

Published in the United States of America

Introduction

People seem to place a lot of importance on first sentences in books, so I'll put this right here and we can avoid that altogether.

Hello, dear reader, it's your old friend, Dr. Cecil H.H. Mills: celebrated wordsmith and oftentimes controversial figurehead in the literary world. You're no doubt browsing through this novel in the Young Adult section of your bookstore, so you may not have heard of my work before. You see, I'm used to having my books placed in the Adult Fiction section. While I may not have done much—or any—research on what exactly constitutes a "Young Adult" reader, I assume that since my old books were placed above a normal human adult's shoulder height, they must have been unreachable to you. Which is fine.

My adult books are very good books, okay? So good that I was inevitably unrestricted by form or marketability. I received carte blanche to let fire flow from my fingers and beauty seep from my pores. It was glorious, the work I could do in my thousand-page tomes. The page was my medium and truth was my ink.

Then some things happened that I don't really want to talk about, and gambling debts being what they are, I found myself taking whatever work the publishers would buy from me. So here I am! Writing a mystery book for adolescent readers! And not a nuanced examination of humanity's descent into the comforting, venomous clutches of technology as the myth of the American dream fades away. I didn't even want to write that anyway. No siree!

Okay, kid, go take this book up to the cashier and buy it so that we can get started.

I'll wait.

Are we good? Did you pay for this? Great.

Now, before we begin the story of the Ghost Hunters Adventure Club, I think it's important that something be said about the Watts brothers, the co-founders of said club. Not about their past, mind you, which remains relatively unimportant and partially expunged from police records thanks to their both recently turning eighteen. I wish instead to talk about them now, in the present, in the hopes that it might give you a hint as to why they do what they do. Perhaps the best way to achieve that is to paint a portrait of them in a specific moment at a specific time:

Currently J.J. and Valentine Watts are puttering up a frigid mountain road as fast as their decades-old motorcycle beneath them will allow. J.J., the eldest by a short amount of time, is at the handlebars and is just barely keeping them from careening into a snowbank. He has a scar across the bridge of his nose. He doesn't like to talk about how he got it.

Valentine, glasses fogged, clings for dear life behind him while he tracks the minute-by-minute loss of feeling in his fingers. He had full use of them once. For most of his life, actually. Riding up a winding road into increasingly inclement conditions is an abstract, rough existence that is a statistical outlier to his usual, more terrestrial rough existence.

(The motorcycle will be ignored after the first couple minutes of the story; however, it's worth knowing that it was received as remuneration following a game of dice and a short fist fight.)

Valentine shouts something that J.J. either can't hear or chooses not to. Probably something about his fingers. Neither are equipped for a ride up to higher altitude, wearing matching sweaters for a reason that will be deduced later by someone smarter than them.

They're almost to where they are going.

Now I'll stop here as I feel that I might be outstaying my welcome, dear reader. That's probably a good primer on these brothers, which, and I can't believe I almost forgot to say this, but it's a little dubious as to whether or not they're actually brothers in the first place. But that will be definitely figured out some other time.

That all being said, it's time to begin the tale of the Watts boys and their crime solving organization, the Ghost Hunters Adventure Club. Now allow your humble narrator to see if he can shut his trap for a minute, switch elegantly to past tense, and let the brothers do the talking.

Act One

CHAPTER 1

An Explosive Beginning

J.J. and Valentine Watts dismounted their motorcycle. Remembering that they had traded the kickstand for gas at the base of the mountain, J.J. laid it gingerly on the snowy pavement near a row of sportscars that might have been driven up in better weather. Before them stood the Grande Chateau, a snowy escape overlooking the cascading mountains a short drive away from Harborville, the boys' hometown. A warm glow was emanating from its windows. Valentine immediately tucked his hands into the armpits of his powder-blue sweater. Perhaps he'd keep his fingers after all.

"Hmm," said Valentine.

"What is it?" asked J.J., shaking the frost off of his red sweater.

"Well, for a place called the Grande Chateau, don't you think it's kind of…regular-sized?"

"C'mon, we'll be late," said J.J. "If someone pays us to solve the Mystery of the Regular-Sized Chateau then we'll go and solve the Mystery of the Regular-Sized Chateau."

"Do you think this guy's serious about the ghosts?" asked Valentine.

"Does it make a difference?"

"To me, yeah."

J.J. warmed up his hands by rubbing them and cupping them over his mouth. He slung his leather satchel around his shoulder. "He's serious enough to pay us, and that's all that matters to me."

Valentine looked up at the sky, noting the approach of dark and billowing clouds.

"Looks ominous," he said.

They did their secret handshake and walked toward the chateau.

* * *

AFTER SNAKING THEIR WAY THROUGH some bellhops and luggage carriers, the two entered the relative warmth of the Grande Chateau's lobby. Inside they found a wide, regal reception room decorated wall to wall with mounted game animal heads, hunting knickknacks, and comfy couches. There was a painting there at the far end of the room—a gargantuan one of a man cradling an ornate hunting rifle, a bested black bear lying lifeless at his feet. Chateau patrons milled around, some lounging and some returning from their ski trips down the mountain. It was barely noon and the bartender was already handing out complimentary glasses of wine as she laughed with the hotel patrons. She had short red hair and an apparently affable demeanor, as far as either of them could tell from this far away.

The boys paused for a moment to stop shivering, then located the front desk and stood patiently behind an older man with a ponytail and sunglasses wearing nothing but a bath towel.

"Listen," said the man to the clerk, "I'm not happy that I'm currently in a hotel lobby in a towel, and that up until a few seconds ago I didn't even have the towel, but sometimes a man takes his breakfast tray out of his bedroom without thinking too far into the future and sometimes he forgets to bring his hotel key."

The clerk had her nose buried in a novel. Appearing close in age to the brothers and wearing a pair of glasses that could make Valentine jealous, she gave nods and "mhms" at regular intervals to create the illusion of sympathy.

"If I could just get a new—"

Without looking up, the woman handed the man a new key. He marched off in a huff, snagging a glass of complimentary wine for the trip upstairs.

J.J. sidled up to the counter and produced a business card. This was his time to shine. "How do you do," he said. "My name is J.J. Watts, and the less-handsome gentleman behind me is my brother and close confidant, Valentine Watts. Together we make up the Ghost Hunters Adventure Club, Harborville's foremost crime-fighting and mystery-solving duo."

J.J. paused for a reaction. The young woman gave him and Valentine a cursory glance before returning to her book. He retracted the business card, peering over the desk to better see the woman engrossed in her novel.

He coughed politely, trying to get her attention. "What, um…what are you reading?"

"No, you're not," replied the young woman.

"Excuse me?"

"Brothers. You're not brothers."

Taken aback, J.J. furrowed his brow. "Now wait a minute…"

"Look," said the woman, closing her book and adjusting her glasses. "You have black hair and brown eyes and your 'brother' has blonde hair and blue eyes. It's rare, but not impossible. Then I noticed that you have detached earlobes while your 'brother' doesn't. Another genetic dissimilarity. If you wanna play the Punnett square game to even the odds, I could see if either of you can roll your tongue."

"Hey, hey, slow down," said J.J. "There's plenty of different ways we could be brothers. We might be adopted siblings for all you know."

"Right, see, that was what I was looking for. Instead of maintaining that you were brothers, you brought up more hypotheticals. You've been thinking about what someone would say if they accused you of not being brothers." She leaned forward, a curt smile appearing on her lips. "That, combined with the matching sweaters, which, I'll add, your friend forgot to take the price tag off of…"

Valentine ripped off the tag dangling from his wrist and stuck it in his back pocket, embarrassed.

"…leads me to deduce that you're not actually brothers, and you're probably just doing this for the bit. Or the brand. Seems like you guys are trying to make money."

J.J. stood there in shocked silence.

"And the book is *Bones of Desire* by Wallace P. Gross," said the woman as she leaned back and began reading again. "Real page turner of a sleuth story."

J.J.'s senses returned to him and he pointed a finger at the woman. "Now listen here you little—"

"Whoa! Let me apologize for my dear brother," said Valentine, jumping between the two. "He was raised by wild animals and failed out of finishing school because he started a fight club. Did you say you were reading Wallace P. Gross?"

"Mhmm."

"He's who we're here to see."

"Oh yeah?" said the woman. "He writes out of the chateau. His stuff's pretty good too, if a little on the nose."

J.J. folded his arms and scoffed. "I'm sure he's a fine author, but he's no Dr. Cecil H.H. Mills. Now *there's* a letter pusher."[1]

"Gentlemen," said a voice from behind them.

The brothers turned around to see an older woman in a sharp business suit and a sour look. Her lapel was embroidered with the logo of the establishment. She extended her manicured hand in greeting.

"Madame Fournier, hotelier of the Grande Chateau, at your service."

---

[1] Editor's note: We were contractually obligated to keep this nod to the author in the book.

"It's sort of regular-sized, isn't it?" remarked Valentine.

"Hmm?"

J.J. accepted the woman's hand. "Please excuse my brother's manners, ma'am. He was a transitory circus performer during his formative years."

J.J. re-produced the business card. "J.J. Watts, the better half of the Watts Brothers and lead investigator of the Ghost Hunters Adventure Club. Charmed to make your acquaintance."

"I'm glad you two were able to make it in before the blizzard struck," she said, accepting and regarding the card with a manner that seemed to give them more credit than they deserved. "If you were out there for another couple minutes you surely would have frozen to death."

"Danger is a core tenet of the Ghost Hunters Adventure Club life-style," said J.J.

"As is neglecting to check the weather report before making a long distance trip," added Valentine.

"Now pardon my manners," said Madame Fournier, "but I couldn't help but overhear you were looking for a Mr. Wallace P. Gross."

"Yes," said Valentine. "He asked us to come up here to discuss business."

"Very well then. Let me show you to his study."

Madame Fournier led the boys up the grand staircase at the end of the lobby and down a long hallway. J.J. tried to sneak in one last hateful glare to the young woman at the front desk, but her nose was still buried in her book.

"Mr. Gross has been a guest of ours for a long while," Madame Fournier told them. "He always comes up to the chateau to work on his mystery novels, which you might know have garnered him worldwide acclaim."

"He always comes up here?" asked J.J.

"Yes, he's a bit of a superstitious type. He wrote his first novel here decades ago and refuses to work anywhere else. He's been at the latest manuscript for the past three years."

The hotelier stopped at a large set of wooden doors and turned to the boys. "I must warn you, however, that Mr. Gross has gotten on in his years and has become a little…eccentric."

"How so?" asked Valentine.

"Well, to start, he just called up two ghost hunters to meet him at a hotel in the mountains."

"Ghost hunters *and* super sleuths," J.J. cut in. "We'll do landscaping, too, if there's a paycheck in it."

"Right. Well, just be warned."

The double doors swung open with an audible squeak and in the center of the room was an old man with frazzled gray hair that stood on end. He stood there, looking distinguished with a tweed vest and knotted bowtie.

"The Ghost Hunters Adventure Club!" he exclaimed. "Please, please, come in."

Madame Fournier took her leave as J.J. and Valentine entered the study, their senses flooding with the smell of rolled tobacco and old hardcovers. The room was lined with bookshelves and enormous, arched windows overlooking the snowscape outside.

Wallace P. Gross walked a circle around the room, gesticulating with an artistic flourish. "J.J. and Valentine Watts. Harborville's finest brother detectives and private investigators! No job too small or too great."

"You've read our website, I see," said J.J.

"I have. You two *are* the brightest minds that Harborville has to offer, yes?"

"Either that or the most search engine optimized," said Valentine.

"I'm sorry, what?"

J.J. coughed. "He meant to say that we're unparalleled in our brightness. We're brightness all-stars. The brightest. Too bright, some might argue."

Wallace rubbed his chin, thinking. "Hmm, right. You'll have to do, then. In that case I must give you the tour."

Wallace P. Gross grabbed his coat and started forward. The boys followed behind dutifully, and the three stepped out into the hall.

"First on the docket," Wallace began, "I'd like to introduce you two to the Grande Chateau. It's a place that I've called home for the past three years now, and a place I've called home many times throughout my life and career. Built over a century ago, this sanctuary was initially meant for Harborville's wealthy elite and urban socialites to unwind from their busy city lives and indulge in their opium-fueled cabalistic indulgences."

J.J. and Valentine shared a glance.

"They had non-opium-fueled cabalistic indulgences too, although that's less important."

The trio rounded a corner and walked into a room filled floor-to-ceiling with books. Gigantic tomes lay stacked on tables throughout, and from the many stained glass windows the boys could see snow coming down at a steadier and steadier rate.

"The library," Wallace said. "That starts with an 'L,' mind you."

The boys, while maybe not smart enough to understand many things, were at least smart enough to know that the word "library" started with the letter "L." They exchanged a confused look.

Wallace went on. "Home to a variety of first editions, encyclopediae, religious texts, and so forth. When not in my study, it is here that I do all of my research for my pantheon of bestselling and award-winning mystery novels."

"It looks very…bookly," J.J. commented.

"Astute observation. Please, please. There's more to see."

Wallace ushered the boys down the stairs and out through the back side of the chateau. They walked out into what must have been a vast and beautiful garden, were it not covered in snow. J.J. and Valentine immediately began shivering in their store-bought, non-woolen sweaters. Wallace didn't appear to mind the cold.

Valentine could see the mountain drop off into a sheer cliff just beyond a winter-worn forest, and a green storage shed stood in the distance.

Clearing snow in front of its doorway was whom he presumed to be the groundskeeper. Even from this distance he could tell that this man stood a head taller than the average man.

"The courtyard," he said. "That starts with the letter 'C.' Are you remembering all of this?"

"It's really cold out here," said Valentine, his teeth beginning to chatter.

A smile spread across Wallace P. Gross's face. "Perfect."

The boys followed Wallace down a snowy path. An old woman in a fur coat and black scarf sat on a bench next to a stone statue of an angel. She didn't seem to mind the cold either.

Looking up at them, her face turned from a scowl to a deeper, more pronounced scowl. "If it isn't my intellectually impotent ex-husband," the woman said.

"Don't look her in the eyes, boys," Wallace warned, the smile sliding from his face. "You'll turn to stone."

J.J. and Valentine glanced at Wallace, trying to assess the validity of his statement.

"J.J., Valentine, I'd like to introduce you to my ex-wife and perennial thorn in my side, Marcella P. Gross."

"Wait," interrupted Valentine, "you have the same middle initial?"

"I took it the same way I took half this man's fortune in the divorce," snapped Marcella.

Valentine gulped.

"Your sense of humor remains sharp," said Wallace. "Whose soul did you sell for it?"

"What..." said J.J., trying to defuse the situation, "...what, um...are you doing out here in the snow, ma'am? It's getting pretty cold out here."

"She wanted to be in a place where her heart felt warm, no doubt."

"What are *you* doing out here, Wallace? Finally looking for a spot to keel over and die?"

"I'll die when I'm good and ready, you frigid ice queen. Come on, boys." Wallace marched toward the chateau.

"It was nice to meet you, ma'am," said Valentine.

"Get lost, Jack."

They entered again through the backside of the chateau, where Wallace led them down another hallway.

"I hope that this isn't being too forward, sir," J.J. said, "but what's your ex-wife doing here at the chateau?"

"You're asking questions that aren't important right now," Mr. Gross replied. He paused for a moment, as if he were either lost in thought or his old man programing had encountered a bug. "That's funny, she was sitting on the bench where we first met."

He shook his head and pressed forward. "Nearly there, come along."

They arrived at a wide room with a vaulted ceiling. A huge chandelier hung above an intricately-woven carpet. Chairs and tables, presumably used for special occasions, were stacked in a corner and also placed haphazardly throughout the room.

"The Grande Ballroom, or Ballroom for short. Starts with the letter 'B.' It's beautiful, isn't it?"

"Lovely," said J.J. out of politeness.

"I didn't want to show it for any other reason than I thought it was nice. Great for dancing. Maybe you two ought to cut a rug in here on your free time."

"We will…put that on the docket," said J.J.

Wallace P. Gross nodded vigorously, his wire-like hair swaying back and forth. "Nearly finished with the tour, gents. This way."

In the hallway, J.J. and Valentine hung back, just out of earshot of the author.

"Are you getting kind of a…I don't know, a 'not all there' vibe from Wallace?" whispered Valentine.

"Was it the casual socialite-cabalistic-ritual dialog or the ping pong match of death threats between him and Marcella that made you think that?"

J.J. sighed. "Look, I'm not personally enamored by the situation at hand either, and I know what you're about to say."

"This isn't right," said Val.

"See? That. I knew you were gonna say that," J.J. replied. "Look, finances being what they are, if we want to eat tonight we're gonna have to at least listen to the guy."

Valentine shook his head. "I don't like that."

"I know you don't. But if you wanna make it in the detective business you're gonna have to take a few bum cases."

They followed the old man back to the chateau lobby and up the stairs to Wallace's study. He closed the door behind them with another squeak from the door's hinges and stood in the center of the room.

"Final stop of the tour," he said. "Study. Starts with an 'S.'"

The boys stood there, waiting for Wallace to say something more. After a moment of wordless smiling, J.J. broke the silence. "So how would you like us to help, Mr. Gross?"

"Ah, yes," said Wallace, snapping back to attention. "As you boys know, I needed the employ of Harborville's finest detectives for a reason. You see," he said, his fingers beginning to tremble, "I'm being haunted."

"Right, ghosts," said J.J. "My brother and I are well-versed in ghost detection and expulsion. However, do keep in mind that we charge extra for poltergeists and ghosts in corporeal form. You pay out of pocket if we have to bring in either an old priest or young priest."

"Take more pride in listening rather than speaking, young man." Wallace's face grew grim. "It might do you some good down the line."

The boys looked at each other, confused.

The author paced around the room, peering out of his window into what had turned into a threatening blizzard outside. "I've known for some time now that a ghost has been watching me. Watching over my latest work. For the past three years I've been consumed by this obsession, this specter, unable to finish my manuscript."

He returned to the center of the room and addressed the boys directly. He heaved a very heavy sigh. "Now I fear my time is short, for I've put together everything and I can see clearly. There are a great many more mysteries to the Grande Chateau than you'd initially believe."

And just as he finished his sentence, Wallace P. Gross's head exploded.

CHAPTER 2

Deputy Park, Harborville Sheriff's Department

Deputy Park burst through the double doors of the Grande Chateau and immediately turned to close them against the roaring blizzard outside. Once he was satisfied that he'd bested the doors in fair and open combat, he kicked the snow off of his boots and brushed the icicles from the ends of his mustache. Unzipping his Harborville Sheriff's Department winter jacket, he marched up the large staircase at the end of the room, where a large crowd of onlookers had gathered.

"Outta the way! Harborville Sheriff's Department!" he shouted, parting through the sea of skiers and hotel patrons grouped shoulder to shoulder. Finally making his way to the front of the crowd, the deputy found the source of the commotion.

"Not you two again!" Deputy Park groaned.

"Deputy Park, our old friend, we meet again," said J.J. He and his brother were sitting in the doorway to the study, wiping their faces and clothes with Grande Chateau-monogrammed towels.

Madame Fournier appeared before the deputy. "Wait, you know these two?"

"Who are you?" asked Park.

"I'm the hotelier of this establishment and the one who telephoned you," she said.

Deputy Park's eyes narrowed. "What's a hotelier?"

"I'm the hotel manager."

"Right," Deputy Park replied, straightening up. "Well it's a wonder your call made it through with the blizzard outside and all." He motioned to the brothers on the floor. "And why is the Ghost Hunters Adventure Club here? Wherever they go, trouble follows."

"*We* follow the *trouble*, you dingus!" J.J. rolled his eyes.

"Oh, is that true?" said Park. "Because every case I run into you two on goes belly up from 'go.'"

J.J. shook his head. "That's not true."

"What about the Old Abandoned Mill?"

"That wasn't our fault!"

"The Harborville Bank Heist?"

"Anyone could have mistaken that old lady for a bank robber."

"What about the Counterfeiters of Pirate's Quay?"

"Hey," Valentine cut in, "didn't we save your life on that one?"

"You did," Deputy Park grumbled, "but I wouldn't have been tied up in that warehouse in the first place if it weren't for you two bumbling idiots." He folded his arms and kicked at the carpet. "Still though, Mrs. Park says…to send you her regards and thanks."

J.J. couldn't help but smile to himself.

Deputy Park readdressed Madame Fournier. "So what have we got here?"

J.J. shot his thumb behind him toward the study. "Dead writer," he said.

Deputy Park turned back to J.J., shocked. "Sweet hollandaise, boys, what have you gotten yourselves into?"

"I called you as soon as I heard the gunshot," Madame Fournier said. "I found these two young gentlemen in the corner screaming when I arrived."

Deputy Park surveyed the scene. In front of him was indeed a dead writer with an exploded head. At the opposite end of the room was a shattered window. Snow was starting to cover the mahogany desk in the center of the room.

"So what happened here?"

Valentine answered. "After the guy talked to us for a while, he took us back to his study, then we heard a gunshot, saw his head explode, and then that glass over there shattered."

"Did you get eyes on the shooter?" asked Deputy Park.

"Sorry," said J.J. "There was a foreign substance in our eyes that prevented us from utilizing the gift of sight."

"What was that?"

"Writer Blood," said Valentine.

Park surveyed the scene once more, brushing his mustache with his fingers in deep thought.

"I've solved the mystery!" he exclaimed.

"Wait, really?" asked Valentine, genuinely perplexed.

"Sure I have," he said, pointing toward the crime scene. "The broken window suggests that the bullet came from outside, ending the life of our dear writer friend here."

He stepped over the body and walked to the window, where the blizzard roared in full force. "Our killer ran away from the scene of the crime and into worsening snow conditions where he'll no doubt freeze to death and die. I'll have Harborville Sheriff's department roll out here with their ice picks to excavate the perp-sicle, avenging the death of Charles Bu-killed-ski over here."

The crowd stood in silence. When no one objected, Park marched to the front of the room. "Welp, just gotta call this one over to headquarters so we can get a slab van to pick up Haruki Murdered-kami. We'll all be outta here in time for dinner." He spoke a few words into his walkie-talkie and waited for a response.

Nothing.

He tried again only to hear static.

"Right," said Park. "New plan. Apparently the blizzard conditions that no doubt froze our mystery murderer have cut off radio communication with the outside world. Which also means that the mountain roads once used to reach this chateau are now rendered inoperable. Looks like we're all stuck here until the roads are clear."

A shocked gasp ran through the crowd.

"Oh, come on," said Park. "We all get to spend the weekend in a snowy mountain resort together and there's only one dead body here which you'll all barely have to see. The killer's long gone."

"We don't know that!" J.J. shook his head. "The killer could be in here right now!"

"Young man, I will karate chop you in the throat," Deputy Park warned. "In any case, the halls will be patrolled by myself, Deputy Jihun Park of the Harborville Sheriff's department." He made a sweeping gesture to the crowd. "No one gets killed on my watch."

The crowd of hotel patrons erupted in chaos and accusatory questions directed toward Deputy Park of the Harborville Sheriff's department.

Madame Fournier jumped between him and the growing mob, trying to defuse the situation. "Please!" she pleaded. "I know everyone here is upset. It goes without saying that all of your rooms will be complimentary for the duration of the blizzard."

The idea of free hotel rooms quieted the crowd down a bit.

A woman with short hair stepped out of the throng. Valentine recognized her as the bartender who was serving drinks when they entered the chateau earlier. "Plus we'll have more complimentary wine after dinner," she said in a thick Bostonian accent.

Everyone in the crowd shrugged and Madame Fournier breathed a sigh of relief.

"Now wait just a second!" yelled J.J., jumping in to join the crowd. "My name is J.J. Watts and the man still picking Writer Brain out of his ears is my brother and indispensable ally, Mr. Valentine Watts. Together we form the entity of Ghost Hunters Adventure Club, Harborville's best and arguably only ghost hunting and crime solving organization."

"Here we go," groaned Deputy Park.

"At the time of his death, my brother and I were in the employ of Mr. Wallace P. Gross, and we will continue to honor his employment request until his killer is brought to justice. And because of this I *will not rest…*" he turned his attention to Madame Fournier, "…until my brother and I are upgraded to a two-bed suite with meals included."

Madame Fournier sighed. "Fine."

"Um, I'd like my room upgraded as well," said a voice. Everyone turned to see that it was the man with the sunglasses and ponytail from earlier.

"No," said the hotelier.

He shrugged. "Worth a shot."

Madame Fournier began funneling the crowd out of the hallway and back down the stairs. "Please everyone, give us some space to clean up a little. I'll have our groundskeeper see what we can do to tidy up here. You all go enjoy a drink in the lounge downstairs."

J.J. and Valentine joined the crowd in their march, avoiding further questioning from Deputy Park. On the way down, they spotted the groundskeeper walking the opposite direction down the stairs. He did, in fact, stand a head taller than everyone else.

CHAPTER 3

The Bookcase

"The real mystery we should be solving is how they got these towels to be so soft," said J.J., rolling up and stuffing as many Grande Chateau-monogrammed towels into his satchel as he could.

They were in their promised two bed suite, an all-oak affair adorned in vaguely rustic knickknacks and landscape paintings of the mountain. Valentine peered out of the window, which would have looked out down into the mountain road that led them here were it not for the howling gale outside.

"We gotta be careful on the way out," said J.J. "I gave the front desk lady a fake credit card for incidentals but she's a sharp one. I didn't help by making the last four digits '6969.'" He looked over at Valentine, whose mind seemed to be lost in the snow outside. "What's the matter? You used to love playing 'steal the hotel amenities.'"

"Do you think Park was right?" asked Valentine.

"I wouldn't trust his opinion on what to get for breakfast, let alone what he thinks about a murder investigation," said J.J. He belly-flopped onto the bed and wrapped himself in high thread count sheets. "But that doesn't matter now."

"What do you mean?" asked Valentine.

21

"I mean that our bankroll had his head exploded. There's no payout for us other than free room and board and whatever you and I can carry out of here undetected."

"C'mon, J.J., you have to at least be a little curious about what's going on here."

"Oh, sure I'm curious. I'm curious about how the upper crust lives, I'm curious to know a weekend without want or need, I'm curious to see if there are any loose gems or precious stones that can be pried and pocketed for later sale." He got up to examine a painting on the wall, noting that it was held in place by a security latch. "I'm not, however, curious about who shot Wallace P. Gross from a sniper's position in a snowy tundra."

"That's the thing," said Valentine, turning his attention away from the snow. "I'm not so sure where the shot came from." He sat on the edge of his own bed. "Try to remember back to when the head exploded. We even told it to Deputy Park. We heard the shot, the head exploded, we got Writer Blood in our eyes, *then* we heard the glass shatter. If the shot came from outside, we would've heard the glass shatter first."

"All right, Sherlock, if the shot didn't come from outside, then where did it come from?"

"I don't know," said Valentine, pointing to his eyes. "Writer Blood."

"Case closed then. Guess we gotta go back to a pampered weekend in a snowy mountain escape."

Valentine furrowed his brow. "If I could just get back to the scene of the crime I could find out for sure."

"This isn't going to get out of your head, is it?" asked J.J.

"No, and I won't stop talking about it, effectively ruining your weekend plans."

"All right." J.J. sighed. "If we can sneak in there tonight and look around, will you let me enjoy the rest of the weekend?"

"I'll even help you strip some copper wire out from the walls."

"Then it's settled," said J.J. "The Ghost Hunters Adventure Club is back on the case, if only for tonight."

The two did their secret handshake to seal the deal.

* * *

THE BOYS WAITED UNTIL MIDNIGHT before they left the room with J.J.'s trusted lockpick kit. By this time they assumed Deputy Park would be done with his rounds, and they made their way from their room, down the elevator, and over to Wallace's study unperturbed.

J.J. knelt on the floor and unfurled his kit while Valentine kept watch at the end of the hall. Selecting the right tensioner and scraping tool was an art that J.J. had long ago mastered. He inserted the tools, ready to work.

The door creaked open.

"Right," said J.J., "another lock successfully picked."

Valentine abandoned his lookout post and joined J.J., where they opened the door and entered with caution, cringing at the squeak of the door as it continued to alert everyone in the hotel to their whereabouts.

The body of Wallace P. Gross was missing. The boys stood there for a moment, trying to deduce what had happened.

"Guess they must've moved him," Valentine concluded.

"Unless he wasn't even dead in the first place, and his headless body now roams these hallways searching for a new head."

Valentine shot a glance at his brother.

"I mean, what if?" asked J.J.

They stepped over the bloody spot where Wallace's body had been and stood in the center of the room. It was covered in a layer of snow thanks to the broken window at the opposite end of the study.

"All right, Inspector Hates-fun," said J.J., "work your magic."

Valentine went to the window and examined the shards of glass at the bottom of the frame. "See? I was right." Valentine pointed to the floor beneath the window pane. "If the shot had come from outside, there would have been glass fragments on this side of the window. Instead it must have been shattered from inside while you and I were blinded by Writer Blood."

"But why would they do that?"

"Maybe to throw us off the trail. To make us think the killer went off and died in a snow storm. Maybe…to make us not wonder if the kill came from inside the house."

J.J. was shivering from the cold. "Look around, we're in a tiny writer's study. Where else could the shot have come from?"

Valentine adjusted his glasses, examining the room. He walked over to the large oak desk that stood as the centerpiece of the room. "That's odd," he said.

"What?"

Valentine brushed away the layer of snow that covered the desk, revealing a stack of books next to Wallace's typewriter, and read aloud, "*Harborville: A Tourist's Guide; An Oral History of Grande Mountain; Advanced Spelunking Techniques*. Was this research material for Wallace's new book?"

J.J. walked over to the desk and opened the drawers. "You ever know a writer type to break a lock and then empty out his drawers?" he asked.

"Why?"

"Because these locks are broken and it looks like the drawers have been emptied. Wouldn't Wallace have kept his manuscript here?"

"Guess so," replied Valentine. "Hmm…"

J.J. had a thought. He went over to the blood spot on the floor and faced his brother. "Val, if you and I got covered in Writer Blood, then that means his head must have exploded toward us. *That* means that the bullet must've struck Wallace from behind."

J.J. turned around and examined the wall by the entrance to the study, feeling over the wallpaper with his fingers. "There!" he exclaimed, before remembering that someone might hear him. "This is where the bullet is lodged." He pointed to a small hole near the frame of the door. "Almost went through one of us. The bullet flew between our heads before we got brain bits in our eyes." J.J. stood by the bullet hole and turned around.

Closing one eye and pointing with a finger, he traced the trajectory of the bullet. "It looks like the shot came from…that bookshelf over there?"

Valentine turned to examine the floor-to-ceiling oak bookshelf filled to the breaking point with leather-bound volumes. "What does that mean?"

"It means we caught the culprit. Cuff 'em, Val, this bookcase will never kill again."

"If what you're saying is true, then there must be something behind this bookcase. C'mon and help me."

"With what?"

"Pull on books. One might open this thing."

"You've gotta be kidding me. That only happens in movies," said J.J. as he pulled on a book that caught a latch and caused the entire bookcase to swing open on a hinge. He shrugged.

"I stand corrected."

Valentine inspected the bookcase and the darkened pathway behind it. "I wonder where it goes."

"Me too. Well, shame that the Mystery of the Hidden Passageway will never get solved. C'mon, Val, let's pack it up."

"What do you mean? We found where the killer took the shot. We gotta go investigate."

J.J. massaged the scar across his nose. "Not happening, bud. I've played unpaid detective for long enough. And to be truthful with you, I don't even think an honest salary would get me to go down that hallway."

"I'm going whether you're coming or not," said Valentine. "Feel free to hang out alone in this spooky study with the blood stain."

"Fine, fine," said J.J., "but if this turns out to be a ghost with a gun, I'll never forgive you."

* * *

VAL LED J.J. PAST THE BOOKCASE and into a stone passageway barely large enough for them to sidle through. Moisture from the air had frosted onto the stones around them. They could see their breath.

"I think I got a cobweb in my mouth," said J.J.

"This passageway must run through the building," said Valentine. "Or maybe it leads to another exit on the other side of the chateau. But why was it built?"

"Wallace did say this building was constructed over a hundred years ago. Maybe it was for the opium," said J.J., running into more spider webs.

The boys continued down the passageway, traversing over cracked stone and rotten woodwork. They could hear faint voices above and around them. The passageway split into different directions just ahead.

"Which way do we go?" asked J.J.

"I guess we follow the sound of the voices."

J.J. sighed.

Ahead of them a slat at the top of the passageway cast a beam of light through the dust.

"That's where it's coming from," said Valentine. "Gimme a boost."

J.J. cupped his hands for Valentine to put his foot into and lifted him up.

"It's a grate, I think," said Valentine. He peered through the slat to see that he was looking into the ballroom Wallace had shown them on the tour. In the center of the room were two figures. Peering closer, he made out Wallace's ex-wife and the ponytailed man with the sunglasses.

"What's happening?" asked J.J., struggling to keep Valentine aloft.

"Shh, Marcella P. Gross and the ponytail guy seem to be mad about something."

Valentine listened intently. The ponytail man was pacing around the room, his arms gesticulating wildly. Marcella was sitting on a chair by a banquet table, coldly smoking a cigarette indoors. She took a long drag and puffed it in his direction.

"People have been suspicious of us," she said. "They've always been suspicious of us."

"Will you just keep a level head?" Ponytail said, sweating profusely. "If you and me just keep quiet and lay low, we'll get through this just fine."

"Something juicy's happening," Valentine whispered down to J.J.

"I'm losing feeling in my fingers," J.J. replied.

Valentine turned his attention back to the conversation happening in the ballroom.

"Let's make sure we're not seen together for the rest of our stay here," Ponytail said. "That should be enough to throw the people off the scent."

"What do you want me to do then?" asked Marcella. "Should I go into open mourning for my ex-husband?" She put out her cigarette directly on the table.

"Maybe wear more black than you usually do. That couldn't hurt."

Valentine looked down again at J.J. "I think these two might have had something to do with Wallace's murder."

J.J. grunted. "I'm dying down here."

"Just a couple more seconds. We might find out something more useful."

Just then, J.J. heard the telltale squeak of the door to Wallace P. Gross's office.

"Someone's coming!"

Ponytail snapped to attention. "What was that?"

"Uh oh," said Valentine. "J.J., be quiet."

Instead of replying, J.J.'s grip broke and Valentine came tumbling down in a loud thud that echoed down the passageway.

"Hey! Who is that?!" came the voice of the man from the ballroom.

Valentine got up off of J.J. and dusted himself off. "What the hell?" he whispered. "We were about to solve the mystery."

"We gotta go," said J.J. "C'mon."

J.J. led him back down the dark hallway, shimmying as fast as they could and ignoring whatever spider webs got into their mouths.

A hand reached out of the darkness and struck J.J. directly on the nose, sending him falling backward onto Valentine.

"Ow!" J.J. looked up to find the young woman from the front desk earlier today. She looked scared, ready to strike again.

"What are you doing here?" she demanded.

"Why did you hit me in the nose?" J.J. demanded back.

"What are *you* doing here?" also demanded Valentine.

The woman lowered her fists. "I...I started wondering about the murder because the deputy's assessment didn't add up. I came to the study and found that the bookcase was open, so I walked in and found you guys here."

"It didn't add up for us either," said Valentine. "The glass was shattered from inside the room, so the bullet didn't come from the outside."

"That's what I thought! You said you saw his head explode *and then* you heard the glass shatter."

"That's the same deduction we came to!"

"Look, everyone," interrupted J.J., "I'm really glad we're all bonding over fine detective work, but we just made a lot of noise and, I think, made some hotel patrons aware of our existence back there. We should probably make ourselves scarce."

J.J. sidled past them toward the study, stopped, then turned to the woman. "Also, we're still not cool, you and me."

They arrived at the study, closed the bookcase, and headed toward the hallway, closing the large double doors behind them.

"Great." J.J. pinched his nose to stem the flow of blood. "Now we just get back to our rooms, shut the door, and put this horror show of a day to bed."

"Hey! If anyone's out there, you should know I have a gun and I'm trained in the art of shooting it!"

"It's Deputy Park!" Valentine hissed. Down the long end of the hallway a shadow rounded the corner. "We have to hide!"

"Follow me!" said the front desk clerk. She dashed forward and led them down the grand staircase. She dove under the reception desk in the lobby and the boys followed close behind. A moment later a beam of light shone over the desk.

"We're *still* not cool," J.J. gasped, trying to catch his breath.

"And you're certain you heard a commotion come from over here?" came a voice they recognized as Deputy Park's.

"Clear as day," said another.

"That sounds like ponytail guy," whispered Valentine.

"You mean Mr. Newbury?" said the young woman.

"Will you two *please* quiet down before we get caught?" J.J. hissed.

"Hey, killer!" Deputy Park called, "if you're here, please come out with your hands up. It's far too spooky right now to be searching every nook and cranny for you."

After a few moments of silence, the flashlight sweeps stopped.

"Welp, sorry, bud. No killers here," Deputy Park concluded. "Might be ghosts, but that's well above my pay grade. Anything spiritually para-normal is something I guarantee you I don't handle well."

The trio waited until long after the footsteps faded off into the distance before they made their way to the elevator. When it reached their floor, J.J. pointed at the young woman.

"Forget our faces," he said.

He and Valentine walked to the safety of their own room. Valentine closed the door behind them.

"That was far too close," said J.J., wrapping himself up in his blanket. "There's no way you're ever getting me to do something like that again."

"Don't you care at all that the real killer's still on the loose? And what sort of shady deal was going on with Marcella and…what's his name, the Newbury fellow."

"Please, Valentine, do us both a favor and just shut your brain off for a minute. It's been a long day and I'm eager to solve the Mystery of What's It Like to Get Eight Hours of Sleep."

"Wait," said Valentine. "Why didn't the study door squeak when we closed it?"

CHAPTER 4

Breakfast

J.J. poured another heaping glob of maple syrup onto his pancakes. "It blows my mind sometimes how these fat cats live. Did you know there's other types of boilings than 'hard?' They get to choose the boiled-ness of their eggs, these bunch of elitists." He glanced over at his brother opposite him in the booth. They were in the Grande Chateau's only restaurant, yet another log-cabin-themed space with plenty of dead animals' heads adorning the walls. Between them lay a breakfast for five. Valentine barely picked at his scrambled eggs.

"What's the matter?" asked J.J. "Your Canadian bacon's getting cold."

Valentine frowned. "The clues just aren't adding up."

"Oh, this again." J.J. rolled his eyes and accepted a refill of coffee from a passing waitress. "What happened to the all-American institution of breakfast? Do these hash browns mean nothing to you? I bet even Sherlock Holmes himself had respect for his sunny-side-ups."

"Sherlock Holmes was English."

"Woulda made a fine American the way he ate those eggs."

"Look," said Valentine, "so much of this isn't making sense. Why did Wallace have that book about spelunking on his desk? Why does this place have secret passageways? Who's going around fixing squeaky door

31

hinges in the middle of the night? Based on what we know, there's still a killer on the loose here at the Grande Chateau, and I'm sorry to tell you this, dear brother, but the whole mystery of it all is affecting my appetite."

J.J. put down the strip of bacon he was eating and sighed. "All right, Val, you want to get into it? Let's get into it. You and I, two sleuths who, despite talking a big game, have never cracked a case, get called up to a snowy resort fortress up in the mountains by an old man with rapidly declining mental faculties. He croaks and the killer is still on the loose. Now, I have it on good authority that the kind of guys who go looking for killers run the occupational hazard of getting killed themselves. So now I'm caught between two diverging paths: one where I go looking for trouble in pursuit of a non-existent paycheck and the other where I mind my own business and spend a relaxing weekend at a place where if you finish all of the bread in the basket a waiter will bring you a new basket of bread for free without you even asking. Eat your breakfast, gumshoe."

All of a sudden, a book slammed down on the table in the only place that didn't have food on it. The boys looked up to see the front desk clerk from the night before.

"You again!" J.J. exclaimed. "I thought we told you to kick rocks."

"Shut up," said the young woman. "This is important."

She tapped the cover of the book.

"*An Oral History of Grande Mountain*," said Valentine. "That's the book that was on Wallace's desk!"

"I thought it was strange that he was reading this, so I went back this morning and snagged it on my rounds. Turns out that when John Henry Grande originally built this place—"

"Wait," interrupted Valentine, "this place was named after a person?"

"Yeah, John Henry Grande."

"So the name of this chateau has nothing to do with the size of it?"

"No. What are you getting at here?"

"Let me apologize for my brother," J.J. cut in. "His favorite game as a child was 'hit the wall with your head.' In any case, we just solved the Mystery of the Regular-Sized Chateau."

The woman sighed. "Let me back up. A hundred years ago this mountain was trailblazed by the wealthy and world renowned explorer, John Henry Grande. It was on this mountain that he built this very chateau that we're all stuck in today."

She flipped the book open to a full-sized picture of a grizzly yet distinguished mountaineer covered in layers of fur, standing at the peak of a mountain.

"Hey," said Valentine, "it's the guy in the painting you see when you walk in."

"Right," said the young woman. "But here's the thing: something happens in his later years and he goes from wealthy socialite to antisocial hermit. He renounces his wealth and status, goes into hiding, and dies alone in his own private Xanadu. Decades later this place reopens as a quaint luxury resort."

"So what's the big deal?" asked J.J. "This mountain has a long and storied history of old men losing their marbles."

"The big deal is what Wallace P. Gross was trying to figure out."

"Oh great, another mystery."

The woman glanced over her shoulder to make sure no one was listening, then leaned toward the two. "Wallace P. Gross was searching for treasure."

J.J.'s ears perked up. "Treasure?"

"I think. See, John Henry Grande renounced his wealth, sure, but no one knows where the money went. Official documents say that it went to charity and his family members, but reading between the lines you can tell something's fishy."

"How so?" asked Valentine.

"Wallace P. Gross wasn't the first person to die on Grande Mountain," said the young woman. She pulled out another book. *Advanced Spelunking Techniques.*

"That was on Wallace's desk, too!" said Valentine.

"I thought it was strange that he was reading this. Maybe he needed it as research for his new book. But then I got to thinking and I went and looked up the statistics on mountaineering-related deaths on Grande Mountain. Surprise, it's abnormally high." She shut both of the books and leaned in further still. "I think the treasure…or whatever Gross was looking for…is hidden somewhere on Grande Mountain, and everyone who's gone searching for it has died."

"Did their heads explode too?" asked J.J.

"No, and that's where this gets interesting. All of these mountaineering deaths can be accounted for, mostly adventurers out of their depth going off trail and falling to their demise. Wallace was different. He *wrote* mysteries so it's pretty clear he liked *solving* mysteries. I think he was trying to crack a code."

"That's a bit of a jump," said J.J. with a raised eyebrow.

"Wallace and I were friends. I liked reading his books and he liked talking to me about them. He'd give me copies and even quizzed me on things after I read them."

"And?" J.J. prompted.

"And then I caught a glimpse of his manuscript. Wallace had been at the book for the last three years and rumor around the chateau was that he'd barely even started it. He was usually extremely secretive about whatever he was working on in there, but this one time I was in his study talking to him and he just had his manuscript out in the open."

"What'd you see?" asked Valentine.

"Only the title. *The Secret of the Grande Chateau.*"

"That could be anything," J.J. scoffed.

"But it could be *something*. Wouldn't you agree it's worth looking into?" The woman hooked her thumb behind her at a person in a booth on the other end of the restaurant. It was the man in the ponytail and sunglasses. "See that guy? That's Thad Newbury. Wallace P. Gross's literary agent."

"What's he doing here?" J.J. asked.

"He checked in the day before Wallace was shot, paid in cash, and was super cagey anytime someone tried to make small talk with him. What I'm thinking is that Wallace was hunting for the treasure of John Henry Grande instead of writing a book."

"And you think Thad has something to do with that treasure?" asked J.J.

"Let's say your ticket to wealth just all of a sudden stops providing and he starts telling you about some great treasure he's on the hunt for. Then maybe you come up here and see for yourself that yes, he's on to the real deal. But what if you start getting greedy and decide to take the money for yourself?"

"The conversation that Marcella and Thad were having last night!" exclaimed Valentine.

"What?" she asked.

"When we found the secret passageway, we followed it down to a vent that overlooked the ballroom. Thad and Marcella were there and neither of them looked happy. Thad said that if they could lay low then they'd make it out fine."

"That's an angle to explore," said the young woman. "Maybe Marcella and Thad were in league with each other."

"Hmm," said J.J., "It *is* funny that they'd both be up here at the same time. But could they kill if it came down to it?"

"It could be possible," said Valentine. "Wallace calls up two private eyes and looks like he's about to blab. Maybe they panic and take things into their own hands rather than risk the info getting into the wrong hands."

"So you'll help me?" she asked.

"Wait," said J.J., "who even *are* you?"

The woman sat up straight and smoothed down her Grande Chateau uniform. "Trudi de la Rosa, front desk receptionist and inquisitive person."

"Well I'm flattered, Trudi de la Rosa, front desk receptionist and inquisitive person, but the Ghost Hunters Adventure Club is closed for business this weekend."

"J.J.," Valentine said, "come on."

"Valentine, my dear brother. Can you join me for a quick Ghost Hunters Adventure Club official sidebar conversation?"

Valentine sighed. "Fine."

They ducked under the booth and spoke in whispers out of earshot from Trudi.

"One, this is dangerous," said J.J. "Two, I was so much happier when all I had to worry about was breakfast."

"You said yourself there wasn't a payday in this gig, but now there's treasure! I wanna solve the case and I know you want the loot. So now we both have skin in the game."

J.J. thought for a moment. Probably about the private island he'd buy if he somehow amassed untold riches.

"Fine. You know the way to my greedy little heart. But how do we trust Ms. Know-it-all up there?"

"I think she's telling the truth."

"She could be waiting to explode our heads herself."

"The Ghost Hunters Adventure Club would outsmart her before that happens," said Valentine, taking into account the fact that they had never cracked a case before, but also that J.J. had a large ego.

"You're right," replied J.J. He sighed. "Are we actually gonna try to solve this mystery?"

"Only if we solve it together."

The brothers popped up from under the table.

"Congratulations, Trudi de la Rosa," said J.J. "My brother and trusted adviser has convinced me to offer you a provisional membership to the Ghost Hunters Adventure Club. Provisional membership entitles you to a Junior Detective title and a Ghost Hunters Adventure Club-branded decoder ring. It does *not* allow you to know the secret handshake."

"What?" replied Trudi. "Join your club? I just came to you two with all this information I had figured out on my own and you want me to be your junior detective? If anything you two should be working for me."

J.J. snorted. "I'd like to see whatever crime solving and ghost hunting business entity you've formed."

"You two are idiots."

"We're two idiots that you need, because we're the only people on this mountain stupid enough to believe what you're telling us enough to investigate it further. You want help figuring this out, you gotta play by our rules."

Trudi tried to reply, but the logic of J.J.'s last sentence was half-baked enough to leave her at a loss for words.

"Now, before we get ahead of ourselves, let's discuss terms." J.J. grabbed a paper napkin and scribbled on it with a pen. "How does a forty-forty-ten split sound to everyone?"

"That's ninety percent," said Trudi.

"C'mon J.J., don't do this," said Valentine.

"One day a legally binding contract written on a napkin will save your life. You mark my words. But fine." J.J. crumpled the napkin then grabbed a new one. "Trudi, your friend drives a hard bargain on your behalf. How about we do a three-way split of revenue?"

"Okay," Trudi agreed.

"Less expenses, of course. I'd really like to buy that motorcycle kick-stand back."

"Sure."

"Then it's settled," said J.J., signing the napkin and passing it around the table for counter-signatures. "Welcome to the Ghost Hunters Adventure Club."

J.J. extended his hand and gave Trudi a firm handshake. Valentine clapped politely.

"So let's plan," said J.J. "We gotta figure out who killed Wallace P. Gross and how they did it. Then we gotta find the treasure. As for the killers, I think Marcella and Thad are our prime suspects."

"Could they have both done it?" asked Valentine.

"Possibly. Or perhaps one could have acted independently of the other. Remember how Marcella was talking to Wallace in the courtyard?"

"It was uncomfortable," Valentine remarked to Trudi.

"I'm aware. She once called me a ghoulish street harlot when I forgot to bring her an extra shower cap."

Over Trudi's shoulder, J.J. saw Thad finishing up his breakfast. He scanned the small group of restaurant patrons to find Marcella on the other end of the room, wearing black, watching her tea get cold from behind her sunglasses. "I think we can find out more if we tail our two friends here."

"What would they have for us other than a confession?" asked Valentine.

"The fact that the locks were broken on Wallace's desk drawers rings alarm bells," said Trudi. "There's a missing manuscript on the loose, and I think they might know the whereabouts."

"We know they were both out late and together last night," Valentine stated, "and that the door to Wallace's study was unlocked. They could have grabbed it easily."

"Right," said J.J., "so I think the logical next step would be to watch these two from afar and see if we can find out where they stashed it."

"Deputy Park is on patrol, though," said Valentine.

"You're right, and the heat's high on us." J.J. directed his attention to Trudi. "Okay, newbie, looks like you got yourself your first field mission."

Trudi rolled her eyes. "Just tell me what I gotta do."

"I'm glad you asked," said J.J. He reached into his satchel and pulled out a hardcover book, handing it to Trudi.

"The Ghost Hunters Adventure Club Field Manual?"

"I had them printed at a vanity press and bought enough to get a wholesale markdown. I figure once the detective business picks up this'll be an amazing ancillary revenue stream." J.J. flipped to the chapter titled *Tailing a Perp*. "Give this thing a read and take notes. There's a short quiz at the end of the chapter, as well as a word jumble that should help you out. But the gist of it is this: keep a safe distance from your target and don't arouse suspicion. You work at this hotel and have the uniform so you should have relatively free roam of the grounds, right?"

"Right."

"Perfect," said J.J., popping one last soft boiled egg into his mouth. "Trudi de la Rosa, you're on the case."

CHAPTER 5

The New Recruit

Trudi de la Rosa had returned to her seat at the reception desk in the lobby of the Grande Chateau. Since the ongoing blizzard prevented new patrons from checking in and old ones from checking out, her job was mainly relegated to fielding phone calls from stir-crazy hotel guests and delivering toiletries to rooms. This only kept her so busy for so long, so she was focusing on her new job—that of being (Junior) Detective Trudi de la Rosa of the Ghost Hunters Adventure Club.

She had reluctantly read the *Tailing a Perp* chapter of the field manual twice, aced the test at the back of the chapter, completed the word jumble, and even did a few of the connect-the-dots puzzles in the other chapters. J.J. wasn't smart, but he made good connect-the-dots puzzles.

On a trip to take fresh towels to a room on the fourth floor, she spotted Marcella P. Gross at her usual position on the bench in the courtyard near the angel statue. She had somehow endured near-whiteout conditions to get to that spot. Trudi couldn't get too good of a read on the woman and what she was doing due to the falling snow, but something about her sagging posture made Trudi deduce that she was sad. She made a note that she would have to research that later.

41

The one person she had trouble finding was Thad Newbury, Wallace P. Gross's longtime literary agent and a man paradoxically in the same location of his client at the time of his death. She noted that he had gone straight to his room after breakfast, and to her knowledge (after repeated checks), he had not exited.

Maybe it was time for another reconnaissance mission.

Trudi set the Ghost Hunters Adventure Club Field Manual under her desk and looked around to see that neither Madame Fournier nor any of the few coworkers stuck up here were paying too much attention. If anyone stopped her, she could just say she was making her rounds.

The Watts brothers were right, this uniform *was* the perfect cover.

She rounded the lobby searching for any clue of Thad's whereabouts, peeking into the restaurant to find nothing. The bar was nearly empty, perfectly reasonable for the early afternoon shift at the Chateau. She thought for a moment about interrogating the bartender to see if she could shed any light on Thad's motives. He was a nightly fixture at the bar and had a penchant for talking. Maybe he had let something slip that the bartender had overheard.

No, it's not the right time for that, she thought. Her nosing around would only arouse suspicion of her at this point. She didn't want the killer knowing she was looking for him. It was best for her to keep a low profile and utilize her eyes and ears. Both of those, coincidentally, were solutions to the connect-the-dots puzzles in the field manual.

With the lobby found clueless, she walked up the grand staircase to see if anything had changed from the night before. The door to the study was closed, of course, and she didn't want to arouse suspicion by snooping around there for clues. Nobody was in the ballroom and Thad wasn't anywhere to be found in the library, only a few hotel guests dying to pass the time until the blizzard ended and the roads could be plowed. For being a literary agent, Thad sure didn't seem to be all that dedicated to reading. Just where could he be?

Trudi thought back to Thad's check-in. She remembered him complaining loudly about forgetting to bring any of his winter clothes to the hotel, as if she could do anything about it. But that meant there was no way he was outside exploring the grounds. And if he wasn't in any of the public areas, that left only one place for him to be: his own hotel room.

Trudi went down the hall and to the elevator, riding it all the way up to the fourth floor. The elevator dinged, the doors opened, and she stepped out.

"P'chew," she said, hugging up against a corner wall. She found that making sound effects made her feel like a better detective. Peering around the corner, she saw Thad Newbury's suite, room 524, all the way at the end of the long hallway. It was time to make her move. She tiptoed the twenty-nine steps to Thad Newbury's room, adding her own soundtrack to the mission as she went along. Past the windows overlooking the court-yard, past the stairwell that could lead her back down in a pinch, and all the way to the very end of the hallway, where she picked up a noise coming from Thad's room.

The closer she got, the louder it got. Was it a conversation?

That doesn't sound like Thad's voice, she thought. *Who could be talking to him right now? Is there even anyone else in the hotel he associates with? Maybe he met someone at the bar last night and they're conspiring right now....* She stifled the urge to squeak. *No time for sound effects now, it's not safe enough.* She checked over her shoulder in case any culprits had snuck up behind her. The carpets were plush and it would have dampened any sound. Nobody was there.

Chancing it, she leaned her ear against the door to hear the conversation as clear as day.

Sports.

Thad Newbury was watching a sports program on TV.

"Aw, man," Trudi said under her breath. Thad spending his day watching TV wouldn't help the investigation get any further.

Dejected, she turned around and slinked back toward the elevator, making sure to create the correct womping footstep sound effects to denote failure. Passing the window, she decided to do one last check on Marcella P. Gross to ensure that her location had not changed. Peering down below to the courtyard, she spotted the familiar black fleck moving through the still-howling storm.

She's on the move! Suspect on the move!

Alarm bells were ringing inside Trudi's head. She had to get to the bottom floor of the Grande Chateau so she could follow the movements of her subject. Deciding in that split moment that it was faster, she dashed for the stairwell at the opposite end of the hallway near the elevator. Trudi made a racket descending all five floors down the echoing stairwell and would have burst out of the door in a noisy huff had she not remembered that the exit was right next to Madame Fournier's office.

Trudi froze when her feet hit the first-floor landing. She caught her breath, smoothed out her uniform, and exited the stairwell with the grace and care of an exemplary Grande Chateau employee.

The coast was clear. Thankfully, no Madame Fournier in sight. Trudi peered across the lobby at the entrance to the courtyard where Marcella P. Gross should be. She barely caught a glimpse of black, expensive fur pass around the corner. Trudi did her most graceful, fastest walk across the lobby. Where could the perp be heading?

Rounding the corner, she caught another dash of black fur entering the elevator.

"Aw, nuts," Trudi said. She speedwalked back to the stairwell.

"Marcella P. Gross...Marcella P. Gross..." she repeated, trying to jog her memory. "What room were you staying in?"

Her memory came back to her in a flash. Marcella P. Gross, room 419. Trudi had checked her in a week before Wallace died at 12:25 in the afternoon. Marcella had remarked that Trudi's uniform was "tacky and boorish," suggesting that she let her manager know for the sake of the rest of the hotel patrons who must have been too embarrassed to mention anything.

419. *That's where she must be going.*

But Trudi had to be sure. As soon as she got into the stairwell, she darted up the stairs as fast as she could. She made it to the door to the second floor and burst out of it, looking toward the elevator banks.

She saw Marcella's elevator. She saw the floor indicator above it, a small arrow turning in a radian from left to right. The arrow reached the second floor, the number two lighting up.

Ding.

The arrow kept moving.

She was still going up.

Trudi dashed up the steps to the third floor, rammed through the door, and shot her gaze over to the elevators.

Ding.

Trudi ran back up the stairs, her heart racing faster now. Fourth floor.

Ding.

Here was the make it or break it floor. Trudi let the adrenaline propel her upward as she made it up another flight of stairs. She opened the door just in time for the elevator to pass.

Ding.

Trudi's thoughts raced. There was one more floor and Marcella didn't keep company with anyone else at the hotel other than Thad Newbury and Wallace P. Gross (deceased). Logically Trudi had to conclude that the only place Marcella *could* be going was Thad Newbury's room.

But, again, she had to be sure. Trudi turned to race up the last flight of stairs. Her heart screamed as she took the steps two by two, summoning her last bits of strength to make it to the final floor of the Grande Chateau in time.

Chest heaving, Trudi de la Rosa burst through the door to the hallway and bounced off of the rotund belly of Deputy Jihun Park, knocking the wind out of herself when she landed on the floor.

"Oh," said Deputy Park. He bent down to help her up.

Deputy Park, whether he knew it or not, was blocking Trudi's eyeline to the elevator banks. She heard a ding. At least she thought she did. Her ears buzzed from exertion and it felt like someone was slicing a cold knife through her lungs. She tried her best to angle herself better so that she could see down the hallway, but the deputy seemed genuinely concerned for her wellbeing.

"Say," said the deputy, "what are you doing running up these stairs?"

Trudi's heart somehow found a way to beat even faster. Her brain screamed for an alibi. Anything.

Come on Trudi, you always have a plan.

"I, um…I like to get a little workout in during my breaks. It keeps me healthy."

This was the most physical exertion Trudi had endured in her eighteen years of life.

Park laughed. "Oh! What a fun idea! It's really important for youngsters like yourself to keep a healthy body as well as a healthy mind."

Trudi nodded politely, trying her hardest to keep her breathing under control. She kept trying as inconspicuously as possible to see around the deputy, but his good-natured talkativeness kept getting in the way.

"What's your workout routine like?" he asked. "I'm always looking for pointers myself."

Trudi thought she caught a glimpse of a fur coat walking down the hallway.

It must be Marcella P. Gross.

"Mrs. Park is always on my case to drop a few pounds. In a perfect world I would start my morning with a proper stretching routine, followed by twenty each of squats, lunges, and push-ups," Deputy Park went on. "In a perfect world, of course."

Trudi's mind went into deduction mode. There was a mustard stain on Deputy Park's left lapel and bread crumbs in the fibers of his uniform; he'd had a turkey sandwich for lunch. His mustache was waxed; he cared about his appearance and must carry wax on his person since he wasn't aware that he'd be staying the night here. One of the buttons on his uniform was mismatched; it must have been tailored recently.

Trudi worked over the information in her mind in a matter of milliseconds. Every moment counted. She had to see if Marcella was going into Thad's room.

"Your, um…your shoe's untied." If she could have smacked her forehead without arousing more suspicion she would have.

"Oh!" said Deputy Park. He bent down to address his shoelaces.

When he kneeled on the chateau's carpet, Trudi was able to see all the way down the hallway. There she was. Marcella P. Gross. She waited nervously at the door to room 524—Thad Newbury's suite. The door opened slightly, and the woman quickly slid behind it, glancing over her shoulder as she went.

It was then that Trudi and Marcella locked eyes.

The door closed as quickly as it opened and Trudi heard the deadbolt lock from all the way across the hallway.

"False alarm," said Deputy Park. "Guess they were tied after all, but I made sure to double knot them just in case."

"I think my break time is just about up," Trudi said. "It was really nice talking to you, Deputy." She moved to make a hasty exit down the stairwell.

"Hold on a second," said the deputy. Trudi froze in place. "There was a commotion last night sometime around midnight. You wouldn't happen to know anything about that, would you?"

"Um…no. I'm not sure what you're talking about."

"I spoke to Madame Fournier today and she told me that you should've been the one running the night desk, only no one was there. If you weren't at your desk, then where were you?"

Trudi turned to look into the deputy's eyes. The friendliness was gone.

"I…was getting my night stairs in."

"Oh!" said the deputy, and he immediately relaxed. "Nothing wrong with a little nighttime exercise. Do make sure you cool down before you go to bed, though. And also be careful around here when you're on your own. The investigation is still ongoing and some people are trying to convince me that the real culprit is a ghost, but with a gun."

Trudi nodded politely again. Once she was on the other side of the stairwell door she released a huge sigh of relief and gripped the railing for support. It took a while for her heart rate to return to normal. She had to tell the brothers about Marcella P. Gross's rendezvous.

* * *

"THERE'S SOMETHING FISHY GOING ON in that hotel room," J.J. Watts said. He paced around the bedroom suite he had secured.

"No duh," replied Trudi.

Valentine turned off the TV. Trudi was leaning against the door to the suite. "So, we got two people acting suspiciously," he said, "telling each other late at night that they can't be seen together, and then meeting in the middle of the day as inconspicuously as possible."

"She caught me looking when she went in," said Trudi. "I'm worried she might think I'm suspicious of something."

"So what do we do?" asked Valentine.

"What we do is we break into Thad's room while he's away and conduct a thorough search," J.J. decided. "Trudes, you gotta have an extra key to his room, right?"

"I mean, I would, if it weren't for the fact that all of the extra keys are in Madame Fournier's office. She'd find out the moment I tried to lift them."

"Got it," said J.J. "Guess we're back to breaking and entering. Trudi, you're still on front desk duty, right?"

"Not for much longer. I'm supposed to be doing my mid-afternoon stairs right now."

"What?"

"That's not important. But yes, I'm off in time for dinner."

"Perfect. All right, Trudi, you're our eyes and ears on the field. At some point Thad Newbury will leave his room for dinner and Marcella P. Gross will presumably go off to some dark corner of the chateau to brood. When that happens, give us a call. Valentine, you're on distraction duty."

"I hate distraction duty," said Valentine.

"I know you do, but we're trying to get some character growth in you. It's when you put yourself out of your comfort zone that you learn about yourself. Plus, the other part of the plan is the breaking and entering, and I know you hate that more."

"True. But what do I do if Thad starts heading back up to his room?"

"I don't know. Pitch him a book idea or something. He's a lit agent after all. Trudi, I'll only need a few minutes to search Thad's room, but I can do it twice as fast with you there. Whaddaya say, cadet? You in?"

"Please stop calling me cadet."

"Splendid. All right, team, let's do this. Trudi, I'm going to need you to turn around for a second so Val and I can do the secret handshake. But do good on this mission and maybe you too will get to learn it."

CHAPTER 6

The Pitch

The phone inside the Watts brothers' suite rang. On the second ring J.J. picked it up and put the receiver to his ear. The voice on the other end of the line was Trudi's.

"Banana," she said.

That was the code word. The mission was a go. J.J. nodded to Valentine, who got up and left the room, taking the elevator up to the fifth floor. Stopping in front of room 524, he took a deep breath, then knocked three times. After a few long moments, a voice came from the other side of the door.

"Who is it?"

"Mr. Newbury, it's Valentine Watts. I think I have some valuable information that you might want to hear."

A longer silence. Valentine's heart beat faster as each passing moment felt like it would be the end of the plan. Then….

"What is it?"

"Sir, I think it might be best if we sat down and had a meal over it, if you don't mind."

More silence. Valentine was ready to call in the abort, which was him leaning his head out of the window and cacawing like a bird so that his brother could hear.

The door swung open, and before him stood Thad Newbury in a button-down shirt with flames at the bottom. He still had his trademark sunglasses and ponytail. He sized Valentine up and down. "You've got five minutes, kid."

Thad followed Valentine silently down the elevator to the first floor. On the way to the restaurant, Valentine spotted Marcella P. Gross smoking in the nonsmoking section of the bar, ignoring the bartender's pleading. He glanced over at the front desk of the reception area and met eyes with Trudi de la Rosa, thumbing his nose at her. She took the cue and left her station to walk toward the elevator banks. She kept her head down as she passed by Madame Fournier talking sternly with the tall groundskeeper.

Once seated, Thad crossed his arms and sighed. "All right, kid, what's so important that you had to drag me all the way down here to talk about it?"

Valentine took a deep breath and leaned in. Thad followed suit. Valentine stared deep into Mr. Newbury's eyes, just past his sunglasses.

"I got a great book idea for you."

* * *

TRUDI KNOCKED ON THE DOOR to the Watts brothers' suite in the prescribed two quick, one slow, two quick fashion that J.J. had taught her. He opened the door as soon as the knocks were done.

"Good to go?"

"Good to go."

They took the elevator to the fifth floor and walked down the long hallway to room 524. Trudi kept lookout while J.J. got on his knees in front of the door and unfurled his trusty lockpicking set. Selecting his trusty scraper and the correct tensioner for the job, he set to work on the lock.

But before he inserted the tensioner, he thought for a moment, put his tools down, and tried the door handle.

The door to room 524 opened.

J.J. frowned at Trudi. "Does nobody here lock their doors?"

* * *

THAD NEWBURY STOOD UP FROM HIS CHAIR.

"Y'know, this always happens. Thanks but no thanks, kid."

"Wait," said Valentine. Thad looked at him expectantly. "I knew who you were from the moment I saw you. You're *the* Thad Newbury. You're a literary titan of the industry."

"Well, 'titan' sounds like a bit of an overstatement."

"Nonsense! The second I laid eyes on you I knew that you were the guy out there making careers happen. Your trademark sunglasses were a dead giveaway. So I say to myself, this is my one chance to get into collaboration with *the* man with the unparalleled eye for literary talent."

Valentine flashed an uncharacteristic smile. "Whaddaya say, pal? Just gimme the time of day and I'll knock your socks off."

Thad sat back down. "A smart person knows when and where they're dumb, and who to ask for help. I think you've got a knack for finding the smart people in the room." He leaned back in his chair. "All right, kid, hit me with what you got."

Valentine Watts truly had not believed he would get this far. He frantically searched around the room for inspiration. "It's…your classic story of good vs. evil," he stumbled.

Thad stared at him with a blank expression.

"And…um…it's about a…" he scanned the room again, spotting a grizzled patron with an eyepatch who looked like he harbored a terrible secret, some animal heads on the wall structured in a way to suggest a long and storied lust for conquest, and a waitress across the restaurant serving coffee whose aspirations obviously laid well beyond her life in the food business.

He couldn't think of anything.

"It's about two brothers," he blurted.

"That's a start," said Thad, still unimpressed. "But where's the conflict? What's the adversity they have to overcome?"

"They're on the run from their past."

Thad sighed. "It's been done before."

"I mean…they're literally being chased by their past." Valentine began perspiring. He had to pull himself out of the tailspin that he was currently in. "Someone from their past is out to get them, to drag them back to the life of lying, cheating, and stealing. She's the embodiment of pure evil."

Thad pinched the bridge of his nose. "So let me get this straight. Your story is about two brothers running from a woman."

"They're…in a gang?"

"Right, they're in a gang. Is there anything they're trying to achieve? Any goal? Something that might have mass market appeal in the thirteen-to-seventeen demographic?"

"Was them being in a gang too much? Does inner conflict count?"

"Okay," said Thad. He got up out of his chair. "I'm clearly dealing with an amateur here. I know we're stuck inside a hotel until this passes over, but *please* don't even think about bending my ear again unless you have an *actual* story to tell. I deal in mystery, I deal in intrigue, I deal in action. I *do not* deal in half-cocked stories about brothers just trying to get by." Thad turned to make his way back to his room. "Don't call me, I'll call you."

"Wait!"

Thad turned with a sigh.

Valentine realized that he was just a hair away from failing his mission. In this moment, he realized something that many young writers fail to figure out and many veteran writers woefully ignore: you have to sell your book by any means necessary. And to do that, sometimes you have to compromise your initial creative vision. Literary agents are not an intelligent bunch, but as they hold the keys to the proverbial kingdom of publishing, they must be pandered to.

He saw Thad's ponytail. He saw Thad's sunglasses. He examined Thad's demeanor. He had an idea.

"The woman…" Valentine said, "what if she had three boobs?"

Valentine cringed. The mission was over. He had to find a way to alert J.J. and Trudi as quickly as possible.

Thad paused in his tracks. That blank expression hidden behind his trademark sunglasses seemed to stare through Valentine's soul. He walked back to the table, sat down, and leaned in. "I'm listening."

* * *

J.J. AND TRUDI ENTERED ROOM 524 and immediately cased the joint. Before them stood a large hotel suite, larger even than Valentine and J.J.'s upgraded suite, with an unmade bed and an open suitcase's worth of clothes strewn across chairs and thrown on the floor.

"Okay," said J.J., "we have two minutes to find what we're looking for and get out of here. I love Valentine, but I doubt that any book pitches he came up with have any commercial viability."

He checked under the bed to see if there were any stray clues lying about. Only dust bunnies. "We're looking for the manuscript, or anything that'll give us a better idea of where it's hiding. Do you think Wallace could have emailed it to him?"

"Probably not," said Trudi. "Wallace P. Gross told me multiple times—unprompted—that he thinks computers are the devil." She picked through the clothes in Thad's closet. "Does this guy only wear button-down shirts with flames on them?"

"There's a few in here with dragons," said J.J. "Check his suitcase. Maybe there's a hard copy of something that'll be useful."

Trudi picked up some of the clothes covering the suitcase on the bed and peered inside. "Here's something," she said, pulling out an old envelope packed full with letters.

J.J. closed the empty cabinet he had just searched and walked over to Trudi. "What is it?"

Trudi thumbed through the letters, reading them as fast as she could. "Looks like correspondences between Wallace P. Gross, Thad Newbury, and…some publishing company called Bradford & Bradford."

J.J. clenched his fist. "Bradford & Bradford, those dirty rats. Never have I met a more dishonest and unkind publishing house."[2]

"The letters get angrier and angrier as time goes on. Seems like Wallace was well overdue on his manuscript and the publishing house had been putting on the pressure. Here's one of Thad Newbury pleading with Wallace to send him something…anything of the new book." Trudi got to the last letter. "Here's something. A letter from Wallace to Thad, dated two weeks ago. 'Dear Thad—'"

"Could you read it in a more blustery, collegiate voice?" asked J.J.

Trudi rolled her eyes. "'Dear Thad, I hope this letter finds you well. As my literary agent and close confidant for the last twenty years, I feel as if I owe you the complete honesty due to a man of your stature. The truth is, Thad, that I've not put a single word of the new novel to ink in the time that I've been at the chateau. Uncharacteristic of me, I know, I'm usually the one client who can scribble out a manuscript over a long weekend. The truth is that I've uncovered something far greater—a mystery in my own backyard that promises untold riches. There exists a secret passage leading beneath the Grande Chateau and I have found the entrance to it behind the bookshelf of my study. Turns out John Henry Grande was a mysterious man who had renounced his fortune and hidden it somewhere in the bowels of Grande Mountain.'"

---

[2] Editor's note: We were contractually obligated to keep this in as well.

"So you were right," said J.J. There was a glimmer in his eyes. He felt like they were on the right track to treasure.

"It keeps going," Trudi said, continuing to read from the letter. "'I've spent my nights exploring the catacomb-like structure beneath the grounds, mapping it thoroughly. There's so much more that I haven't yet been able to solve, but I'm hoping that by the time I see you next, I'll have more to report. The mystery is nearly solved, my dear Mr. Newbury. Until our next correspondence, Wallace P. Gross.'" Trudi placed the letter back where she found it. "There's no more letters after that."

"Thad must've come straight up to the chateau after he got this letter. Makes sense. Maybe something went wrong with the two between then and when his head exploded."

"That still doesn't explain Marcella's involvement."

"True." J.J. thought for a moment. "It could be what triggered the murder in the first place. Maybe Thad and Marcella had a prior involvement where they knew they could get rich off the old man if they offed him."

"Maybe," said Trudi. "Or maybe they found out he wasn't as off the rails as they thought he was and they decided to grab the money for themselves."

J.J. placed the pile of clothes back on the suitcase. "Luckily neither of them can leave until this storm blows over, so we've got time. For now, though, I think I know where we need to go next."

CHAPTER 7

Exploration #2

Valentine closed the door to their room behind him and breathed a huge sigh of relief. He found J.J. and Trudi waiting expectantly for his return.

"How'd it go?" asked J.J.

"I think I might have just secured an advance for a three book series." Valentine plopped face-down on the unoccupied second bed and heaved another sigh. "Turns out odd-numbered boobs are a hot seller in the market."

"What?" asked Trudi.

Valentine rolled over. "It isn't important and I'd like to scrub the preceding hour's conversation from my brain as soon as possible. What'd you guys find out?"

"Wallace and Thad and their publisher, Bradford & Bradford, were in a heated go-between for the better part of three years over a past-due manuscript," Trudi reported.

J.J. scoffed. "Bradford & Bradford, those buffoons. They wouldn't know true art if it punched them in the nose."

"Anyway," said Trudi, "Gross had actually been spending his time researching the treasure of John Henry Grande. Said he was close to finding it and he just needed a little more time."

Valentine raised his eyebrows. "You were right! So what happened next?"

"Then Wallace P. Gross's head exploded and we found ourselves snowed in at a chateau with a suspicious-looking literary agent and a venom-filled old crone, both of whom either have very valid reasons to kill a writer or have verbally stated their projected enjoyment of killing said writer."

"You keep the letter?" asked Valentine. "It could be useful evidence in case we need to take this to the police."

"Negative, gumshoe," said J.J. "That letter would do a better job of convicting us of breaking and entering than it would of solving this mystery. We've got more evidence to collect."

"So what's next?" asked Trudi.

J.J. reached into his satchel and produced three flashlights with the initials of the Grande Chateau monogrammed on them. "We're going exploring."

"Where'd you get those?" asked Trudi.

"Can you believe people just leave these underneath a desk and behind a locked cabinet, available for anyone to grab?"

Valentine sat up. "Are we going back into the secret passageway?"

"You betcha. We only saw the part of the passageway that led to the ballroom. I'd bet Vegas odds that there's more passageways to more parts of the chateau if we spend a little more time down there mapping it out. And who knows, maybe it'll lead to the treasure."

"Wallace had been searching for years and still came up short."

"A head short," said J.J.

"Stop it," said Valentine. "I don't think finding the treasure is as simple as sneaking around some spooky secret hallways. But you're right. Maybe there's a clue down there."

"So when do we go?" asked Trudi.

"Tonight. Midnight. And hey, de la Rosa, could you do me a favor?"

"What's that?"

"For the love of Christmas, please don't punch me in the nose again."

* * *

THE TEAM ARRIVED AT THE STUDY just past midnight, after everyone had gone to bed. A night manager was sleeping upright at the front desk. It didn't take much sneaking for the three to get past him.

J.J. didn't even bother bringing his lockpick set. He turned the handle to the study's door and they walked right in. The squeak was still gone.

But the room was in a worse state than before. The blizzard had made its way in through the broken window and had claimed the desk as well as the rest of the floor. A light dusting of frost had covered the bloodstain where the body of Wallace P. Gross once was.

Valentine walked up to the bookshelf at the far end of the room and wiped snow off of a shelf of books. "Which was the one you pulled again?"

"That old novel by Dr. Cecil H.H. Mills. You know, the one that was way ahead of its time?"

Valentine brushed the cover of a weighty tome, unveiling the name of the extraordinarily intelligent and extremely handsome author.

"*Cerberus, From On High*," Valentine read.

"What a phenomenal piece of art," said J.J.

Valentine gave the book a pull and a latch gave way behind the bookcase. The entire apparatus swung on a hinge, and the more Valentine pulled, the more it revealed the small passageway behind it.

"Ghost Hunters Adventure Club, this could be a dangerous mission," said J.J. "This could even be our last mission, depending on what's down there. So I'm gonna need everyone on the squad to stay frosty. That goes double for you, newbie."

J.J. pointed an accusatory finger at Trudi, who rolled her eyes.

"Just stick to the plan and remember to meet up back at the hotel room in case any of us get lost," J.J. continued. "Valentine, I'm gonna forgo the usual secret handshake due to current circumstances. But just know that I'm secret handshaking you right now in my mind."

Valentine nodded. "Ready?"

"Ready," Trudi and J.J. chorused.

They each turned on their flashlights and entered into the curved stone archway before them. Valentine immediately began shivering as they walked deeper into the passage. The beams of the flashlights fell off into the darkness before them.

"Here," said Valentine. "This is where we turned to find the vent overlooking the ballroom."

"And where we overheard Marcella and Thad talking about their plans," said J.J.

"Do you think there could be anyone there now?" asked Trudi.

"Hmm…" J.J. scratched his chin because he thought it was the right thing to do to make him seem smarter than he actually was. "It'd be a good idea for us to go and check it out."

But the ballroom was vacant.

The team walked back to the fork in the passageway and went to the second path. It sloped downward, and their footsteps disturbed the dust and ice on the floor. Valentine coughed.

"Shh…" said J.J., "we don't know who could be listening in on us, or even where in the chateau we could be."

The passageway grew smaller and smaller until it ended at a ledge leading downward. They peered over the cliff made out of long-rotted wood, their flashlights illuminating a stone-cobbled platform just beneath it.

J.J. shook his head. "Not it."

Valentine sighed and got down on his knees, sliding down onto the lower platform.

"I'm gonna go check this out. If I don't come back, remember me as a man who died doing what he loved."

"Here lies Valentine Watts," said J.J., "dude loved asbestos poisoning."

Valentine dusted himself off and walked down the passageway just beyond the sights of Trudi and J.J.'s flashlights. They waited, listening to Valentine's footsteps grow more and more distant.

"Trudi, you know you get promoted if he dies."

"Guys, come over here!" Valentine's voice came from down the hallway.

Trudi and J.J. worked their way down the ledge and followed the sound of Valentine's voice to where he was standing. To his left was another passageway leading off into darkness, but before him was a solid wall made out of the same cobblestones that surrounded them.

"Congratulations," said J.J. "You found a wall."

"Not just any wall," Valentine replied. "Look here."

Trudi and J.J. peered closer at two small holes in the cobblestone spaced inches away from each other. Dim light leaked from the other end. Squinting, they honed in on the front desk manager snoring at his desk at the other end of the room.

"It's the chateau lobby!" exclaimed J.J.

Trudi pulled back from the peephole. "We must be looking through the eyes of John Henry Grande. The ones in the huge lobby painting."

"Precisely," said Valentine. "Whoever built these passageways must have used them to spy on the guests. I'll bet you there's more vents and peepholes looking out into different areas of the chateau."

"But why?" asked Trudi.

"Beats me," Valentine said with a shrug. "It's starting to sound like John Henry Grande was as strange as Wallace was. Maybe that's why the author admired him so much."

"Two paranoid dead guys aren't gonna get us any closer to finding this treasure," said J.J.

"But it might give us an idea of why he hid the treasure in the first place," said Trudi. "We should keep searching these passageways to see if there's any more clues here."

They trudged onward, now having to hunch down to keep from hitting their heads on the low ceiling. J.J. accidentally swallowed and spat out more centuries-old spider webs.

The Ghost Hunters Adventure Club mapped out the secret passageways thusly: there were the lookout vents in the ballroom and in the lobby, of course. Traveling further into the labyrinth they discovered spying ports through the base of an ornate candelabra in the library. There were additional viewports in the kitchen and bar areas of the lobby. The passageways snaked through the walls of the chateau, providing vantage points to every common area.

"Why don't any of the passages go into the sleeping areas?" asked J.J.

"Maybe that wasn't John Henry Grande's angle," Valentine surmised. "I'm getting paranoid vibes from the guy, not creep vibes. There's a huge difference."

They followed the pathways until they reached one final corner. Trudi reached out to feel a frigid draft.

"Is this the exit?"

"Only one way to find out." J.J fought to stop his teeth from chattering. "Remind me to put in an order for Ghost Hunters Adventure Club-branded parkas when we get down the mountain."

They pushed forward, following the pathway down deeper into the darkness. Any light that had seeped in through peep holes or cracks in the wall had vanished behind them and before them the hallway sloped off further down toward a slatted metal grate barely visible in the distance. The echoes of their footfalls on hard stone gave way to soft clunks of wood. J.J. looked down to see fresh snow blowing in from the direction in which they were heading.

"This must lead out to the courtyard, based on where we are," said Trudi.

"Hey, how old do you think this wood is?" J.J. asked.

The rotten planks gave way beneath the trio and sent them tumbling downward. The three screamed as they plummeted the short drop and landed with a thud on the floor beneath them. Trudi coughed as dust shot up into the air.

"Where are we?" Valentine asked between wheezes.

They got back to their feet and shined their flashlights around them. Directly in front of them stood a large stone door with carvings on it. Behind them appeared to be a corridor.

"Ah sweet," said J.J., "a sub-secret passageway. When you're adventuring you're lucky enough to find just one secret passageway. But when you come across two? That's pay dirt." He walked up to the corridor behind them and shined his flashlight on it. The path had been partially obstructed by wooden poles running horizontally from either wall. J.J. peered further in. "Hey, have either of you ever seen a real human skeleton? Like, not a fake one but one that definitely looks real and like it's been rotting for a while?"

Trudi and Valentine cocked their heads at him.

"Because I'm pretty sure this is one of those."

The three adventurers grouped together at the mouth of the corridor and shined their lights through the wooden poles. Sure enough, there were the bones of a man propped standing up, the poles through his ribcage keeping him upright. What clothes hadn't rotted away hung in tatters off of his body.

"Gnarly," Valentine commented.

Trudi studied the skeleton intently. "He must have been an adventurer searching for John Henry Grande's fortune. There," she pointed, "he stepped on a pressure plate walking through this corridor and…" her finger rose to the wooden poles. "Yep, spears to the chest."

"A booby trap," said J.J.

"Looks like it. I guess we already solved this particular puzzle."

"It looks like he was heading toward this door behind us," Valentine said. "I guess by falling through that wooden floor upstairs we must've dropped in partway through this labyrinth."

J.J. whistled. "John Henry Grande, you continue to surprise me every day, you rich, eccentric, booby-trap-building man." He walked back to the center of the room. "Welp, onto the next puzzle."

"Wait," said Trudi, "we could get killed down here."

"Killed upstairs by a murderous lit agent or crushed in the catacombs by an ingenious trap…what's the difference? There's treasure this way. Plus, we're the smartest detectives Harborville has ever seen."

"How true is that?" asked Trudi.

"Anyway," said J.J., as he inspected the stone door at the other end of the room, "looks like there's an inscription here." He brushed the dust off of the coarse stone of the door, revealing words finely engraved into it. "'To you, adventurer who seeks my riches,'" he read aloud. "'I have traveled the world and learned its secrets that I may never repeat to another living soul. I have designed this labyrinth so that only the truest of seekers may find my treasure. Good luck, I say to thee, and may you find what you are seeking.' This fella had a thing for theatrics."

"There's another inscription down here." Valentine shone his light at the lower right hand corner of the door. In much cruder handwriting than the previous inscription was another message:

BEWARE THE MONSTER AT THE END OF THE MAZE

"Looks like it was carved by a knife."

Valentine took in the room again, examining the walls for any other inscriptions that might help them. On the leftmost wall he spotted rows of small holes spaced uniformly apart. Inspecting it closer, he counted ten rows down and four columns across. He couldn't see further than an inch or two down the holes when he shined his light down them. Raising his hand up, he made to probe one of the holes with his index finger.

"Hey, look at this," said J.J.

Valentine turned to follow the beam of his brother's flashlight. Just below the inscription, a small clearing was made at the bottom of the door by a wooden pole.

"I guess somebody propped it up," said Trudi.

J.J. crouched down and pointed his flashlight under the opening in the stone door. The beam fell off just feet away, revealing nothing but loose gravel on the ground. "Well, at the very least the hole is Val-shaped."

"Wait…" said Valentine. "You're not telling me I should—"

"Come on." J.J. got up and dusted the dirt off of his pants. "You said you wanted adventure, and you got some claustrophobic-looking adventure right there."

"I'm not gonna…no, of all the dumb ideas you've had…I'm not gonna crawl into the abyss. We should come back more prepared."

"With what? You want me to call up the Ghost Hunters Adventure Club-branded excavation team? You want me to see if I can drag over my boy Drew from the docks to haul his industrial crane up here? No. Especially because me and Drew aren't on speaking terms anymore. I hope he's well."

"Whenever we gotta do anything dangerous you always volunteer me for the job, J.J.," Valentine whined.

"Okay, smart guy, name *one* time when I put you in danger."

"You lowered me into shark-infested waters with a crane on the dock job!"

"First of all, it wasn't even shark season, so you weren't in *mortal* danger. Second of all, I just realized why Drew and I don't talk anymore."

"Guys, I made it," Trudi's voice came from the other side of the stone door. J.J. and Val dropped to the floor to spot her flashlight beam scanning the new room.

"Trudi!" J.J. exclaimed. "Exemplary showcase of courage and conviction under fire. I'm sure some *other* members of the Ghost Hunters Adventure Club could learn a thing or two from your can-do attitude."

Valentine flicked a pebble at his brother's face. J.J. responded by punching him in the arm. Valentine punched him back. J.J. put Valentine in a headlock and demanded that he say "uncle" before letting him go. Valentine broke the headlock by punching J.J. in the stomach. This was a thing the two regularly did.

"Trudi," said Valentine, "what do you see?"

They heard shuffling from the other side of the stone door. The light from her flashlight swept under the door, illuminating the boys' faces.

"It's a huge room," she said. "I can't see the end of it."

The pebbles crackling under her feet grew fainter. "I'm gonna go see what I can see."

"Be safe, I guess!" said J.J.

The two brothers stood and dusted themselves off before sitting up against the wall.

"Wanna take bets on whether or not she'll come back?"

Valentine shot a glance at his brother. "Do you ever, for just one moment, take anything seriously?"

"What? I'm plenty serious."

"We just fell through a trap door into a secret cavern that might have treasure at the other end of it, if it doesn't kill us first. I'm not asking you to lose your patented J.J. charm, which has gotten us arrested a non-zero amount of times. I just think maybe you should quit trying to lighten the mood at every chance you get. It's unbecoming of a gentleman."

J.J. thumbed his nose and coughed up a bit of cave dust. He sighed.

Time passed.

The sound of Trudi's footfalls could no longer be heard.

Valentine asked his brother, "You good?"

"Yeah. You good?"

"Yeah."

J.J. slid back to the ground and shone his flashlight under the crack of the stone door. He could see nothing but dust particles suspended in the air.

"Hey, Trudi?" he called.

He waited for an answer.

"Trudi!"

No response came.

"Valentine, what should we do?"

Before Valentine could respond, the boys heard the faint patter of feet from the other side of the door, growing louder and louder.

"It's her!" exclaimed J.J.

"She's running," said Valentine. "Why is she running?"

The footfalls grew louder until Trudi slid to the opening of the door. Their flashlights illuminated her panicked face.

"Get me out! I'm not alone down here!"

Behind her and in the distance they heard a soft scraping noise. Metal against rock. *Shunk. Shunk. Shunk.* It grew louder. It was getting closer.

The brothers reached out their hands and grabbed hold of Trudi. She dropped her flashlight and took each of them by the wrists.

Shunk. Shunk. Shunk.

The noise was nearly on top of them.

"Pull!" yelled J.J.

The stone door was a tight fit, but the fear and panic of the situation made pulling Trudi through the hole that much more difficult. The noise was right behind her.

Something grabbed her leg and she screamed.

"It's got me!"

J.J. and Valentine pulled harder against the unseen assailant. It was tug of war and Trudi was the rope. Valentine felt like they were losing her as she was pulled back further from the stone door.

"You gotta do something!" yelled J.J. "Give it a kick, kid!"

Trudi took her free leg and kicked with all her might against whatever was holding her. She flailed wildly, kicking again and again. A loud grunt echoed through the cavernous room when she connected with what she could only assume was a face.

For a brief moment she saw the man's hand gripped around her leg before it released. A body rolled backward onto the ground behind her.

"I'm free!" she yelled. The brothers pulled one last time and dragged Trudi through the small hole created by the propped up stick. As she slid through she knocked the pole propping up the door out of place and the stone door slammed shut with a resounding thud.

Trudi, Valentine, and J.J. panted for breath on the floor of the secret passageway. Valentine felt as if he was about to have a heart attack.

"I try my hardest not to swear," J.J. said between gasps for air, "because I think anyone who can't find the proper words to use in a situation out of all the words in the English dictionary might lack a certain sense of creativity..." He got up to his knees and pointed at the stone door. "But what the *hell* was that?"

"I don't know," said Trudi. "I was exploring the room. It was huge and I couldn't find another exit. I got to the other end when I heard what sounded like digging. As soon as I got close it stopped and footsteps were walking toward me. That's when I ran back to you guys."

"Well, whatever or *whoever* it was, I think we just locked it in there," said J.J.

Valentine nodded. "As long as they're not strong enough to open that door."

J.J. glanced at the other two. "We should probably go, huh?"

They dusted themselves off and climbed their way carefully out of the trap door they had created for themselves. They retraced their steps out of the stone passageways leading back to the chateau and through the secret entrance in Wallace's study, making their way back to the boys' room without seeing anyone. Luck was on their side. At least some of the time.

CHAPTER 8

A Hypothesis

"Well, it could've been worse," J.J. said, locking the door to their hotel room at the Grande Chateau. He pushed a wooden desk up against the door for added safety. "We coulda lost the new recruit, and we all know how pricey it is to find new talent after you've trained the old one."

"That's not funny. We could've died twenty different ways down there," said Valentine.

"Yeah, and the number one complaint of any human resources department of any business is how costly the hiring process is. We should all count our lucky stars. In any case, what'd we learn tonight?"

"There's a secret passageway that lets you get to any part of the chateau undetected," said Trudi, "and beneath that is another secret passageway that has a bunch of booby traps."

"Wallace P. Gross must've been down there," Valentine surmised. "He could've been the one to prop open the stone door in the first place, if he already knew about it."

"We can't be sure if that was him," J.J. said. "That's sloppy police work. Thad or anyone else who knew about the secret passageways could've gotten through that door if they knew about it."

"Plus it doesn't really seem like they 'solved' the puzzle," Trudi said. "Brute forcing a door and keeping it propped up doesn't seem like a Wallace thing to do."

"There was a panel of holes on the side wall," Valentine remarked. "Maybe that could've been key to solving it."

J.J. looked out the window at the still-roaring blizzard. The weather hadn't let up and only appeared to be getting worse, from the looks of it.

"Here's a hypothesis," he said. "What if the person who grabbed you in that cavern was Thad?"

"Where are you going with this?" asked Valentine.

"Hear me out. Thad knew about the secret passageway thanks to Wallace's letters. It makes sense that he would find the passageway beneath the chateau. Perhaps in a different way from how we found it, but it's not entirely unreasonable that he could come across it. So he spends his nights solving the puzzles down there with the help of Marcella, who might not be strong enough to open a heavy stone door, but is definitely smart enough to avoid getting impaled by spikes."

"It'd explain why Marcella meets with Thad," said Trudi. "And it makes sense that they would want to avoid arousing suspicion."

"That must mean we left Thad down there in the cavern," said J.J. "Unless he's strong enough to get through that door or smart enough to finish the puzzle to get out of there without dying."

"He wouldn't try to," said Valentine. "'A smart man knows when and where he's dumb and who to ask for help.' He said that to me when I was pitching *Boob Quest* to him."

"*Boob Quest*?" Trudi echoed.

"It's not important. Look, if that's Thad and we really did trap him down there, he's smart enough to wait for Marcella to come down and rescue him."

"If we can pin down Thad in the secret cavern and then have Deputy Park find the correspondences between him and Wallace in his room, that has to be enough for an arrest," said J.J.

"But what about Marcella?" asked Trudi.

"But what about Marcella indeed."

J.J. thought for a moment. "All right, Trudes, I've got a mission for you. Marcella P. Gross has been way too suspicious and obviously knows something we don't. We need you to find out what that is."

"Why me?"

"It's taken me all of two days to realize you could probably crush both of us with your mind if you truly felt the desire to. Marcella's got a whip for a tongue and might try to trick you into selling your soul to the devil in exchange for a blues guitar, but if anyone's got a shot at interrogating her and finding out exactly how and why those two literary types offed Wallace, it's you."

Trudi nodded. "I can do it."

"That's the Ghost Hunters Adventure Club spirit!"

"But *how* should I do it?"

"A very good question," replied J.J. "One that I don't know the answer to. Frankly—and this is me being vulnerable with my truths here—but frankly I'm afraid to even look at the woman."

"You could try to appeal to her sensibilities," Valentine suggested. "Maybe there's some common ground you two could find that would make her trust you."

"You don't, perchance, have a gland in your mouth that spits acid as self-defense, do you?" asked J.J.

"No," Trudi replied, "but I think I can figure something out."

CHAPTER 9

The Parlor Accusation Scene

S itting at the front desk of the Grande Chateau, Trudi yawned. The events of the previous night had been exhausting and she stayed up even longer trying to figure out what to say to Marcella. She ended up studying the Ghost Hunters Adventure Club Field Manual's section on advanced interrogation techniques, since it was the only literature on it she had.

She scanned the lobby. No sign of Marcella P. Gross; however, she spotted J.J. and Valentine Watts in the back of the restaurant having breakfast. J.J. had his usual stack of pancakes, waffles, eggs, bacon, Canadian bacon, and turkey bacon that he ordered off-menu. He had on a dumb fedora that he'd lifted from the lost and found, wore it tilted, and peeked out at her as inconspicuously as possible from behind a newspaper. She could tell he was keeping tabs on her, in case anything were to go wrong and he had to, in his own words, "throw elbows."

The blizzard raged on outside. From last she heard it should be ending soon, but it blew with the same ferocity now as it had the night before. Even when it ended it wouldn't be over. The denizens of the Grande Chateau would then have to contend with the gargantuan snow drifts before they could finally get down the mountain.

The team had spent the entire morning trying to locate Thad Newbury. Going up to his room and listening through the door proved fruitless: not even sports on TV. None of them spotted him in the common hallways of the chateau. J.J. held on to the theory that they had locked Thad in the secret passageway beneath the chateau that led into the mountain the night before. If that were the case, they would have to solve the mystery soon, or else another person's life could be at stake.

The elevator dinged and Marcella P. Gross stepped out in a black dress, black fur coat, black fur hat, and a set of white pearls as accent. She marched in a direct line toward Trudi, whose heart began racing. She had expected that she would have to track the writer's ex-lover down later in the day, hopefully with enough time to come up with a better idea than the none she had. Beads of sweat began to form on her brow as the woman arrived at the front desk.

"Good morning. I've come to once again complain about the amenities of this establishment."

Trudi's eyes darted back and forth in search of a response. She caught eyes with J.J. from across the room. He nodded encouragingly from behind the funny pages of the newspaper.

"What…what seems to be the problem, Ms. Gross?"

Nice. Good start, Trudi.

Marcella let out a long sigh. "Once again your hotel staff has placed my bedsheet in such a way that the tag is at the head of the bed. It doesn't take a world class establishment to know that the tag is meant for the foot of the bed. How am I supposed to get my rest if I have to spend half the night stripping my bed and rearranging my sheets?"

Here was an in if Trudi ever saw one. "You know," she said, "I've yelled at the housekeeping staff on more than one occasion about their lack of attention to detail when it comes to bedsheet tags, Ms. Gross. I don't care if they're freshly washed. That side of the bed is where feet go and I'll not hear another word of it."

Marcella raised an eyebrow suspiciously. "I'll bet."

Deciding she needed to drive this further home, Trudi leaned in for effect. "I even once caught them putting on pillowcases inside out. Unforgivable!"

Marcella couldn't help but gasp at the thought of such cavalier attitudes toward hotel amenities. "Well I hope you give them yet another tongue lashing for my sake. The *nerve* of some people when it comes to bedding."

"Ms. Gross, it will not be the first time and may regrettably not be the last. But give me time and resources and I'll have this chateau in proper working shape as soon as possible."

"Thank you," Marcella said in the tone one takes when they finally feel understood. She turned to leave but doubled back upon a thought. "I may have been wrong about you. I initially took you for an apathetic teen without a care for hospitality, but you've got a good head on your shoulders."

Trudi saw her window open and knew it would close in moments. It was now or never.

"I know much more about this place than I usually let on."

Marcella's eyes narrowed, her trademark coldness coming back in full force.

"Is that so?" she said, closing the distance between them. The desk was the only thing to protect Trudi from Marcella's overbearing presence.

"I think I can help you with your current predicament, if help was what you were looking for."

Marcella's eyes became slits. She was smart enough to know that Trudi wasn't talking about hotel amenities anymore. "Choose your next words carefully, girl. There's no telling if they could be your last."

Trudi couldn't help gulping at the threat. In a cracked voice that betrayed her lack of confidence, she said, "Beware the monster at the end of the maze."

The ex-lover's eyes widened and she drew back with a gasp. "What… are you even talking about?"

"Listen, I know things you might already know, and I know things you definitely don't know. I know you and Thad have been in league, but I think I have something I can add to the team if you would let me. Maybe we could help each other."

Marcella's expression changed from one of confusion to one of shock to one of anger in the space of moments. She drew back and slapped Trudi with all her might. Trudi gasped in pain.

"Don't you *dare* try to butt into my private affairs!"

The entire lobby full of patrons fell dead silent upon hearing the slap. Everyone looked in their direction. Trudi felt her face grow red in equal parts pain and embarrassment.

"Welp, my time to shine," said J.J. He threw his newspaper down and tossed off his fedora, leaving the restaurant area and neglecting to pay for the breakfast or even charge it to another room.

Valentine finished his orange juice and followed. He had no idea what his brother was doing, but knew from experience that he didn't want to be left alone with a breakfast bill.

Letting anger overtake her, Trudi drew back her fist, aiming straight for Marcella P. Gross's jaw.

"Everyone! Everyone! Could I have your attention please?" J.J. stood near the top of the grand staircase of the lobby, managing to turn everyone's attention from Trudi and Marcella to him. "Gather around everyone! I have an important announcement to make!"

The patrons of the Grande Chateau slowly formed a semi-circle around the base of the stairs. Everyone looked around to each other quizzically.

"Is everyone here? Yes, yes, keep gathering around. Don't be shy."

Valentine joined up with the semi-circle of patrons and looked around to study their faces. He spotted Deputy Park looking like steam was about to blow out of his ears. Madame Fournier and the rest of the hotel staff stood around with confused looks on their faces. He spotted the groundskeeper wiping dirt off of his hands. He spotted the twenty other hotel patrons who had been snowed in with everyone else. He did *not* spot Thad Newbury.

"Yes, even you two." J.J. motioned over to Trudi and Marcella, who both reluctantly joined the crowd at the bottom of the stairs. "Right, yes, thank you, everyone, for joining me this morning in the place where we're literally all stuck. As many of you know, tensions have been running high at the chateau due to the untimely demise of our dear friend and my post-humous client, Wallace P. Gross."

Deputy Park groaned. "Here we go again."

"Yes, thank you Deputy Park, here we do go again. The reason why I've called you all here at the base of these steps is because I've solved the murder."

A shockwave of gasps rolled through the crowd and the guests whispered to each other.

Madame Fournier pushed her way to the front to reach J.J. "Just what is the meaning of this?" she demanded.

"Justice, Madame Fournier."

The hotelier looked angrily toward Deputy Park. "Why are you letting these children whip my hotel patrons into a panic?"

"They pull shenanigans like this all the time," said the deputy. "They won't shut up until they get whatever it is off their chest. We might as well just let them get it over with."

Madame Fournier folded her arms and huffed. "They're making a mockery of my fine establishment."

"A mockery, yes," said J.J. "Let's all have a good laugh at how quickly the Ghost Hunters Adventure Club solved the mystery. The Ghost Hunters Adventure Club, Harborville's foremost private investigation unit, available at a discount if you bring in the coupon from our website. Act now and get thirty-three percent off of our Ghost Hunters Adventure Club-branded merchan—"

"Oh, come on, get on with it already!" shouted Deputy Park.

"Pardon me, Deputy. This is the first time I've gotten to do a classic Agatha Christie-style parlor accusation scene and I'm relishing in the opportunity."

"Child, I will karate chop you in the throat."

"That may be the truth, and I daresay I invite you to try, old man, but please allow me a moment of your time. I promise it will be worth it once you've heard my story."

Deputy Park folded his arms and let out a grumpy harrumph.

"Splendid. As I was saying, just a few short days ago our dear Wallace P. Gross was cruelly wrested from this earthly plane."

J.J. motioned with a dramatic flourish to the study at the top of the stairs and down the hallway. He started up the last few steps and headed down the hall toward the large, wooden double doors that once kept Wallace and his work from the outside world. "This way, this way, don't be shy," J.J. said to the crowd.

Trudi made her way to the front of the group with Valentine.

J.J. stood in front of the doors. "Behind this door is the answer to the Mystery of the Grande Chateau. The answer to how and why our Wallace P. Gross was murdered."

J.J. had them all by the ear now, he knew it. He threw open the double doors and stepped into the snow-covered room, taking care to avoid the frosted stains of blood on the floor. "According to our hard-working-yet-ultimately-incorrect friend of the police state here…" J.J. said, motioning over to Deputy Park.

"Watch it," Park replied.

"…Wallace P. Gross was supposedly shot from *outside* the chateau. Note the shards of glass that should have broken *toward* us, and how they had actually been ejected *out* of the window which…" J.J. peered out through the broken window and onto the snowdrift below. "…has thusly been obscured by elemental efforts beyond our control. Excellent."

The whole crowd had joined J.J. in the study, some flowing into the hallway outside. J.J. could feel that he was beginning to lose them with his failed evidence reveal. He had to razzle with the rest of the evidence from here on out.

"Now, presupposing our correctness with the glass until such a time affords it that a state-sponsored forensics team can confirm it, let's move forward with a timeline of events. One: Wallace P. Gross invites my brother and me on a tour of the Grande Chateau. Two: he leads us into his study. Three: his head explodes, covering both my brother and me in Writer Blood and incapacitating our natural talent of sight.

"So I ask you, if not from outside, how could Wallace P. Gross have been shot and killed from behind closed doors with only myself, my brother, and Wallace P. Gross in the room?"

"We haven't ruled you two out yet," Deputy Park said with tired indignation.

"When we found them here they were raving in a panic, shouting, and, I quote," Trudi piped up, "'Oh no oh no his head exploded! What's going on? What's in my eyes? Is that Writer Blood?'" She adjusted her glasses for dramatic effect; one of the suggestions in the Ghost Hunters Adventure Club Field Manual was to always have a prop to work with when making dramatic gestures. "In any case, they were drenched in Wallace's blood. Even a rudimentary blood spatter analysis would suggest that Wallace was shot from behind them."

"Fine," said Deputy Park. "Would you please hurry it up?"

"Okay, okay." J.J. paced around the room in a long arc as he spoke, rounding the desk to the bookshelf behind it. "The question here, as with all other great detective stories, is not who did it and how, but *why*. Let me warn you fine folk of the Grande Chateau that the killer, or should I say *killers*, are here in this room and among all of you right now. And their names are…"

He pointed with an accusatory finger and summoned his adult accusation voice.

"Marcella P. Gross!"

A shockwave of gasps rippled through the crowd, who all turned toward Marcella. Her mouth fell agape. She readied herself to speak, but J.J. beat her to the punch.

"And her accomplice was none other than Thad Newbury! Wallace P. Gross's literary agent!"

More gasps from the crowd, who had become more than accustomed to performative gasping by this point. They all turned their heads to spot the second accused, but could not find him anywhere.

"I bet you're all wondering where Thad is," said J.J. with a smirk. "Here's where things get interesting." J.J. leaned against the fake book-shelf. "What no one knew during the initial investigation was that between the walls of the Grande Chateau exists a vast network of secret passageways that lead to different rooms and a bevy of spying vantage points throughout the common areas."

An actual, literal gasp escaped from the crowd at this point. They spoke amongst themselves, wondering what strange things they thought the killers had seen them doing under assumed privacy.

"Don't worry," J.J. assured the gathering, "this isn't a sexy spying thing. At least not in this case. You see, if the gunshot didn't come from outside, then it had to come from somewhere. And that somewhere was right before our very eyes, hiding in plain sight." J.J. pulled on the Dr. Cecil H.H. Mills book with a grand flourish.

It fell to the floor.

He took a deep breath. "Valentine, that was the right book, right?"

"Uh…yeah," said Valentine.

"Well, that certainly took the wind out of my sails." J.J. began pulling on all of the books he could get his hands on to, ejecting them from the bookcase and onto the floor. Nothing caused the bookcase to magically swing open as it previously had. He grabbed either side of it and tried shaking it like a vending machine that had done him wrong, but nothing budged. Turning around in a huff, he addressed the perplexed crowd.

"Okay, so you're just going to have to take my word for it that there's a secret passageway behind this door that Marcella P. Gross and Thad Newbury used to assassinate Wallace in order to take not only his wealth, but the wealth of John Henry Grande that Wallace had recently discovered."

"Hold on just a minute," said Deputy Park. "You can't just run around and accuse someone of murder with absolutely no evidence to back it up."

Marcella literally clutched the literal pearls around her neck. "How could you accuse me of...why in the world would you...?'"

J.J. jumped back onto the offensive. "Listen, I know I can't absolutely prove it right now but you *have* to take my word for it that there's something behind this bookcase. I don't know why it isn't opening, but if you give me enough time I'll find out."

"You outstayed your welcome two botched cases ago," said Deputy Park.

"Valentine and I were back there. We explored further into the secret passageway with Trudi from the front desk over there. Tell 'em, Trudi."

"You did *what*?" Madame Fournier shrieked.

Trudi shrank herself down in the crowd, her face turning red once again.

"I had suspicions that you were leaving your post at night, but I had no idea you were using that time to sneak around the chateau and pester guests."

Trudi stared down at her feet, not knowing what to say but definitely understanding that silence was a valid option here.

"We will discuss this later," said Madame Fournier in a decidedly "you will be fired" kind of tone.

J.J. felt his grip on the situation loosening. "The night of Wallace P. Gross's murder, we overheard a heated conversation between Marcella and Thad. Do you remember that conversation, Ms. Gross? 'Let's just make sure we're not seen together for the rest of our stay here. That should be enough to throw people off the scent'?"

Marcella stared, mouth agape, at J.J. This was perhaps the first time since he had met her that her expression betrayed her usual ice-cold demeanor. Tears were welling up in her eyes.

"And just where is Thad?" said J.J. "Well, it turns out that there was more to the secret passageway than we had initially thought. And who else should we find down there but Thad Newbury!"

"Did you actually see him, or is this another one of your half-truths?" asked Deputy Park.

"Well, we didn't *see him* see him. It was dark and we were being chased. But we managed to escape his grasp and trap him in one of the rooms of the underground passageway.

"And that's why," J.J. said, feeling like he was winning over the crowd again, "if you look around right now you'll note that everyone here is present and accounted for *except* Thad Newbury. Where is he, I ask, if not trapped underground after having murdered Wallace P. Gross and then using his manuscript to try and steal John Henry Grande's fortune from right under all of our noses?"

"Wait," said Deputy Park, "even if I believed you, which I guarantee you I don't, did you literally just admit to trapping someone and allowing them to freeze to death in an underground passage?"

"Yes," J.J. said, but immediately went on to qualify, "but it was a life or death situation that left us with no other choice. Plus, I think the insulation was pretty good down there, don'tcha think, Val?"

"It was pretty good insulation," Valentine said, nodding.

"What are we all talking about?" Thad Newbury said from the back of the crowd. The entire group of hotel patrons craned their heads to see the man in nothing but sunglasses and a towel.

"Well, well, well," said J.J., trying to spin this in his favor. "If it isn't the man of the hour. How'd you escape from the stone door?"

"How'd I escape from the what?"

"Don't play dumb with me. We know that you murdered Wallace P. Gross in order to obtain his wealth and the wealth of John Henry Grande."

"I did *what*?"

"The jig's up, Thad. You and Marcella conspired to kill Wallace. You knew about the secret passageways. We have evidence to back this all up that you didn't hear on account of you coming here late because you finally escaped from under the stone door and then, I guess, took a shower."

"Jeez," said Thad, "A guy wakes up late and takes a shower and walks outside forgetting his room key and this is how he's treated?"

"But you weren't in your room," Valentine said. "You always keep sports on the television, even when you're sleeping. This morning it wasn't on. You only turn it off when you're not around."

"You…are correct," said Thad. He began visibly perspiring.

"So where were you, book boy?" asked J.J.

"I was…I was…" Thad stammered. He looked around the room at all of the inquisitive faces of the patrons of the Grande Chateau. His eyes darted from person to person, searching for anything that would help him.

"Fine! I'll confess!"

The sea of patrons parted to reveal Marcella P. Gross, tears streaming down her face.

"He was with me," she said, her voice a crackling, sobbing mess. "In my hotel room. We've been having an affair."

It was J.J.'s turn to gasp dramatically. "Whaaaaaat?"

"Well, I suppose it wasn't exactly an affair. Wallace and I have long since been divorced. But if he ever found out, I knew it would destroy him. That's why I've been keeping it under wraps for so long."

Thad Newbury hung his head in shame. "It's true."

"Ah, jeez…" said J.J., pinching the bridge of his nose and wincing. "That's what you meant when you said 'let's just make sure we're not seen together for the rest of our stay here.' You two were knockin' boots."

"We were romantically intertwined, yes," said Marcella. She sighed deeply, looking around the room. "Wallace even delivered a note to me the day before he died. At least I think it was him. It was in his handwriting but it was cut in half. I couldn't make out what it said. It's probably just Wallace being his usual self, thinking that his life was a mystery novel." She wiped the tears from her eyes. "I…regret how I treated him. If only I could speak to him one last time." Summoning her courage, she put on a brave face that resembled her usual scowl. "Now that my indiscretion has been exposed to the entirety of this chateau, am I free to go?"

J.J.'s face felt hot. "No further questions, ma'am."

Deputy Park took control of the room. "Okay, not that I was holding anyone here, but you're all free to go about your day and do whatever it is you've been doing. I think I might sit down to brunch myself if anyone's interested."

The entire crowd began dispersing out of the study and back down to the lobby. J.J. discreetly tried to join his brother in the crowd, avoiding eye contact with Deputy Park.

"Except for you two," said Deputy Park, grabbing the brothers by their collars. He squared up to the two boys, puffing out his chest, and looked like he was ready to explode. "I've long since had it up to here with you two, but this is a brand-new level of trouble you boys have gotten into."

"We were just trying to help," Valentine said in their defense.

"Help?" Deputy Park scoffed. "The only thing you two helped do was to embarrass a widow in front of an entire chateau's worth of people. I hope you're both proud of yourselves."

"Listen—" said J.J.

"No, *you* listen, you little punk. This is a real life crime scene, and your all-American boy detective act has done nothing but make things worse and potentially have you committing more crimes. This is your last warning. If I even catch a whiff of you two trying to snoop around, I will throw you off of this mountain myself."

CHAPTER 10

Interlude

Well, it would appear we're far enough into the book that I can assume the literary agents and early reviewers have stopped reading by this point, so I think that affords us time to have a little chat.

Hello, reader, it's me, bestselling author and 1985 record holder for most swear words used in an interview in one minute, Dr. Cecil H.H. Mills. I hope you're comfortable wherever you're reading this, whether in your favorite comfy chair, at the library, or in the event that this book has lasted into the near future, on your allotted six minute break underground in the salt mine that the robots have forced you to harvest. They can't harvest it themselves because the salt corrodes their circuitry. Remember this and rise up!

I'm where I've been since the last time we checked in, still tapping away happily in my snowy mountain escape in the woods. I've been here for the last few weeks and have been enjoying my lack of human contact. The only people I've talked to so far are the mailman, the gentleman at the corner down the way, and the sock puppet I created for whenever I feel the overwhelming need to scream at someone.

There is one other person, though. I see him infrequently and always at night. He stands at the edge of the woods on my property, just far enough in the brush to obfuscate his face and body. He doesn't move, even when I shine a flashlight on him. But when the light bounces back at me, I always see a flash of steel. Is he holding something in his hand? Why does he stare at me? Is he staring through me?

Sometimes I wake up at night to a light scratching at the windowsill in my bedroom. Metal against glass. I'm too paralyzed with fear to move, so I just lie there and listen. The scraping turns to tapping. Tap. Tap. Tap. Eventually the tapping becomes a whispered voice.

"Cecil, Cecil, come outside," it says. "Come pay for your sins. It's easy, Cecil, you just have to unlock your door and come outside."

I'm sure the two things are wholly unrelated, but just in case they might not be I figured I'd mention it. I should leave something for him in case he gets hungry. Maybe he likes baked bread.

Anyway, reader, I'm sure your time is as valuable as mine, so let me try and make this chapter useful for you. In case you have to write a book report on *Ghost Hunters Adventure Club and the Secret of the Grande Chateau*, I'll just go ahead and tell you the things you need to know to make it as easy as possible.

The theme of this book is that children are idiots.

Now before you go writing angry letters to me, dear reader. Dear, sweet reader. Beloved, beautiful, darling reader that I cherish. You paid for this book. And for you to do that I believe puts you an intellectual cut above the rest.

You're cool. Keep up the good work, buddy.

The Watts brothers, however, should not be trusted to tie their own shoes, let alone go and solve a mystery. By this point they have committed so much obstruction of justice that it would supply enough material for a different crime-solving duo to take them down in a brand new series of detective novels. The very instance of them entering a crime scene the way that they did would, by letter of the law, render all of that evidence inadmissible in court. Their actions are reckless, dangerous, and all-around incompetent by any rational person's standards. This book exists as a cautionary tale to all of you who read it, so that you may avoid the mistakes caused by and befallen unto these two half-wits.

But hey, adventures sell books, right? That's what the kids want to read, right? At least according to my lit agent, that's what they want. Kids these days don't want the real page-turners. Not like the books of yesteryear. No publisher would take my 1,003-page treatise on the human condition or my collection of short stories exploring interpersonal interconnectedness through the lens of a man who saw the future—but only as far as the next time he farted. So here I am in my cabin punching out boy detective novels on my time-tested Remington Elitra I once bought in a thrift store that had strange symbols from some Baltic state.

Feel free to mention all of that in your book report.

Let's give you some easier things to write about. The motorcycle I mentioned in the first chapter that I guarantee you will not come up again in this or any one of my other books was missing its kickstand. Feel free to write a five hundred-word essay about how that missing kickstand represents a fractured sense of shared self between the brothers.

The scar on J.J.'s nose that he doesn't like talking about represents a past he's running away from, that I'm running away from, that we're all running away from. You can cite this section of the book as a primary source because I, the writer, am telling you what it means. If you try to suggest otherwise I will phone your teacher and argue for a lower grade. I guarantee I have the time and enough impotent rage to do that.

What else? Hell, let's move on to other books in your curriculum. The green light at the end of the harbor in The Great Gatsby represents Jay Gatsby's love of marijuana. The grapes in the *Grapes of Wrath* represent the pair of stones that John Steinbeck must've had to expect me to read all the way through that snorefest. Holden Caulfield is a whiny baby and you can't even play baseball in a field of rye.

Hold on, my phone's ringing.

I walk over to the one rotary landline telephone in the cabin, my only electric connection with the outside world. The phone rings three times before I pick it up.

"Hello," I say.

"Mr. Mills, it's me, J.J. Watts."

"I know," I say. "Because I'm the one writing this right now. I'm having the conversation in my head and I'm putting it into a typewriter. I know it's a little metaphysical but please try and stick with me."

I hear silence on the other end of the line and remember that I forgot something. "Also, it's Doctor Mills. Remember I have a doctorate."

"Right, so anyway you probably know why I'm calling being that you're the one holding the reins, right?"

"You're calling because you're at a dead end and you need some hints to solve the mystery."

"Exactly."

"Well, I'm sorry, son. I'm not running a wayward home for lost sleuths here." I pull the receiver away from my ear and begin to put it away, knowing full well that J.J. isn't done here.

"Wait!"

I put the receiver back to my ear.

"Cut me a little slack. This is our first book and we're in a pretty rough spot. I tried to do the parlor room accusation thing but it completely backfired and—"

"And you made an old lady cry. I know. See, kid, your problem was that you were too quick to come to a conclusion and you let that drive your detective work, making you bend clues to fit your own narrative. This is Sleuthing 101 here."

There's a long pause on the end of the line, then, "Yeah, I guess you're right."

"So maybe you just have to look at things from the beginning. All the clues are there. I'm very good at foreshadowing, you know."

"I know, I know, but listen...neither you nor I want this book to be any longer than it needs to be. I know you're not getting paid by the word, so if you don't want to write fifty extra pages of my brother and I shaking each chateau patron down one by one in the most boring, monotonous way possible, I think that it would benefit everyone if you pointed me, Valentine, and Trudi in the right direction."

I sigh. "Here's the thing. I don't know how the book is gonna end. Honestly, I didn't even think I'd get this far. It's a miracle I could type out this many pages of young adult fiction without throwing my typewriter into a river."

"Surely you must have written an outline before you started."

"Outlines are for cowards."

I hear a long groan from J.J. and some loud thumping noises. He doesn't tell me what that is but since it's all coming from my head I'll let you, the reader, know that J.J. was repeatedly kicking the desk I supplied for him and his friends in their upgraded suite.

"Listen, youngblood," I start, "I'm only gonna say this once and I don't want it to read as if I have an ounce of kindness in my body, but what you, Valentine, and Trudi lack in textbook detective skills you make up with your indomitable spirits. I built you three to be tougher than whatever life can throw at you, and together you kids could take over the world. I know you're feeling pretty frustrated right now, but that's how midpoints work in traditional three-act story structures. Don't give up."

I listen to the receiver, knowing full well J.J. isn't the sort of character to receive sincerity and return with sincerity.

"Blow it out your corn cob pipe, doc."

There we go.

"Listen," I say, "I'm gonna hang up now because if this chapter gets too long it'll get caught by whoever's job it is to give my work a light skimming before it goes to print. Take care, kid."

I hang up the receiver and walk back to my Remington Elitra situated at the window of my cabin. The man is back again at the edge of the woods. He looks like he's in better spirits today.

Now, where was I?

Act Two

CHAPTER 11

A New Plan

J.J. placed the phone back on its hook and sighed. "Well, that was useless."

"What'd he say?" asked Valentine. He and Trudi sat on the bed behind J.J. in their room.

"Just some writer-y crap. Something about the dominance of the human spirit or whatever. Nothing that actually helped." He walked over to the other bed in the room and face planted onto it. "Well that's a dead end for me. I'm ready to go back to my original theory of 'Ghost, but with gun.'" J.J. dragged his face from the comforter to face the two. "Trudi, what happened to your nametag?"

Trudi looked down at her blouse, noticing the rectangular pattern where stitching had been removed. "Madame Fournier called me into her office and fired me. Told me that if she found me snooping again she'd have me arrested. But I got to keep the dress since it came out of my paycheck."

"Good thing you have your detective career to fall back on," said J.J.

Trudi glared with the appropriate amount of hatred for J.J. "I should never have gotten involved with you two."

"I should mention now that technically we only pay in exposure," replied J.J. "We also don't offer any health insurance. Legally, Ghost Hunters Adventure Club is a religious organization and you're gaining volunteer hours that should look pretty good on a college application. But no, I will not write you a letter of recommendation."

"I'm sorry that happened to you," said Valentine, showcasing the assumed northern limit of human understanding that existed between the two boys.

"Whatever," said Trudi. "I can't change it now."

"So I guess we're back to square one." Valentine sighed. "We're no closer to catching the killer than we were on day one."

"Catching the killer *and* finding the treasure," said J.J. "Please don't forget about the treasure."

"You sure can't stop thinking about that treasure, can you?" Trudi remarked.

"Someone has to keep their priorities straight."

Trudi idly examined the ceiling of their hotel room. "There has to be something we're missing. What if we looked at things again from the beginning?"

"All right," Valentine agreed. "A few days ago, J.J. and I got a call from Wallace and then we rode up here on our motorcycle."

"No, even further back. When did Wallace first become obsessed with John Henry Grande?"

"He said he'd been coming here since he wrote his very first novel. He even met his wife here. I think he first mentioned the treasure in that letter to Thad, but must've known about it long beforehand."

"What if finding the treasure was what he considered to be his last mystery?" J.J. spoke up.

This conjecture lit a spark in Trudi's brain. "Or what if *we* are his last great mystery?"

J.J.'s ears perked. He pushed himself up and sat on the bed. "What do you mean?"

"Think about it. His ex-wife and agent are at the chateau in time to witness his death. He called two private investigators up the mountain to be around when he dies. He knew about the coming blizzard—he could've timed it all out perfectly knowing full well he was gonna die, but he'd have the right people and the right clues to figure out who killed him."

"That sounds a bit far-fetched," said J.J.

"I thought so too, until I remembered it was the plot of his third novel."

"What?"

"I mean, there's some differences. The detective in the book didn't make any old ladies cry, but it doesn't seem so far-fetched when the idea came from his brain before. Ever since I started working here, Mr. Gross would give me his books to read. I didn't think anything of it and I read them because I didn't have anything else to do, but the weird thing was that he would regularly quiz me on the books."

"So you could be a part of the puzzle too," said Valentine.

"I could be. I don't know. All of these coincidences happening at once is starting to make me feel like they weren't coincidences at all."

Valentine looked out the window onto the chateau grounds below. The snow had finally stopped beating down, but the damage had been done. He could barely make out the edges of the road that had brought them up the mountain.

"In the morning the snow plows will clear the roads and the real murderers will get away," he said. "Wallace knew the snowstorm would give us time to solve the mystery, but we're running out of time."

"Think back to when you first met Wallace," said Trudi. "If he was giving me clues then he must've been giving you two clues as well."

J.J. thought for a moment. "The first thing he did when he met us was ask us whether we were as good of private investigators as we said we were. Naturally I embellished. But then he took us on that strange tour."

"Wasn't it weird that he made a point of telling us the first letter of each location?" asked Valentine.

J.J. nodded. "Library, Courtyard, Ballroom, Study. 'LCBS.' What could that mean?"

"There were plenty of coded messages in all of Wallace's mystery novels," said Trudi, "it could be directions, a keycode, or even an acronym."

J.J. thought hard. "Loners Can't Be Sorry…Lousy Coffee Brings Serendipity…Look, Counting Backward Sucks. That last one is pretty true, don't you think?"

"What about the note Marcella received from Wallace before he died?" asked Valentine. "The one that she can't read. Maybe it has something to do with that."

J.J. groaned. "I'd like to cordially request that we pursue other avenues than speaking to Marcella. Right now she's liable to rip my still-beating heart out with her bare hands after the stunt I pulled."

"Let's give that some breathing time, yeah," said Trudi. "Is there anything else we can go off of right now?"

Valentine stared out of the window, deep in thought. With the flurry now died down, he could make out the far-off lights of Harborville down at the base of the mountain. He searched his mind and ran through the tour with Wallace over and over again.

"There is one thing," he said. "When Wallace was showing us the ballroom, he said something peculiar. 'Maybe you two should cut a rug in here sometime.'"

"We thought he was just being his regular brand of eccentric self when he said it," said J.J., "but what if it was a clue?"

"So he wants us to go and do a dance number?" asked Valentine.

"It's worth checking out. And to be honest it's much more preferable to having my head bitten off by an emotional widow who just had her infidelity broadcasted to a chateau's-worth of people."

"I'm game," said Valentine. "It's the only direction we can go in right now."

"What about Deputy Park?" asked Trudi. "His threats—plus me getting fired—mean we're all red-lined. If he catches us snooping around we're all in a world of trouble."

"I'm not too worried about it. By this point in my life I've done a master's thesis on avoiding cops," said J.J.

"It's actually one of his better talents, if you can call it that," added Valentine. "Eighty percent of his brain is dedicated to mapping the cops in the vicinity and memorizing their schedules. Where's Park, J.J.?"

"He's about to sit down for dinner. Usually orders a medium-well steak with a baked potato. When he feels like he's done a good job, he opts for seafood. Without fail he'll make bad puns to impress the waitress. She's not amused by it."

"See?" said Valentine. "It's magic. So we just wait until dinnertime and we'll have complete access to the ballroom. It's trying to figure out Wallace's cryptic clues that'll be the challenge."

J.J. hopped up from the bed. "And so, beaten but not broken, the Ghost Hunters Adventure Club once again embarks upon their quest for untold riches."

"And Wallace's murderer," added Valentine.

"And Wallace's murderer," parroted J.J. "The trio, not knowing what trials lay before them, are steeled by the knowledge of their unmatched intelligence, cunning, and in the case of J.J. Watts, bewildering good looks."

"We've reached your self-narration quota for today," said Valentine. "Are you guys ready?"

"Ready as I'll ever be," said Trudi.

"Trudi, it's time we teach you the secret handshake," J.J. said. "The condensed version. You can't handle the long version yet—it's too future. But when the time comes, you'll know."

CHAPTER 12

The Ballroom Puzzle

J.J., Valentine, and Trudi opted to take the stairs down to avoid sharing an elevator with any third parties who might be suspicious of them roaming the chateau together. Luckily, the dinnertime crowds had left the second floor at the top of the grand staircase empty and undisturbed. J.J. crouched against the railing and peeked over the grand staircase. From his vantage point he spotted the top of Deputy Park's head, seated in the chateau's restaurant.

"Looks like he's starting on appetizers. We've got plenty of time."

"Madame Fournier isn't around here, is she?" asked Trudi. "I really don't want to be arrested."

"Doesn't look like it, kiddo," replied J.J. "But being arrested isn't so bad. You should try it sometime."

The trio snuck over to the ballroom doors. J.J. kept his lockpick set in his satchel, just in case; but knowing the rule of threes in comedy, he figured he wouldn't need them.

And he was right. The doors swung open to reveal the empty ballroom.

"We can work with this," said Valentine.

Trudi closed the door behind them and they wandered in, taking stock of the place. There were chairs stacked against the far corner of the room, some circular tables with chairs dotting the walls surrounding them, and a beautiful crystal chandelier hanging above them in the center of the ballroom. The room was cast in a warm glow by the electric candelabras affixed to the walls.

"Hold on," said Valentine. He looked around the room, trying to picture it in his head from a certain angle. "Thad and Marcella were having their conversation right here…" he said, creating a frame with his thumbs and forefingers. "So that must mean…" He turned directly behind him and pointed toward a small vent at the top of the wall. "We spotted them from right here."

Trudi and J.J. joined Valentine to examine the vent. What should have given them a small vantage point into the secret passageway was now covered from the inside.

"Looks like plywood," said J.J.

"It makes sense, right?" Valentine said. "Whoever the real killer is must've known that we were down there and sealed the entrances. It had the benefit of making you look like a damn fool when you tried to accuse Marcella and Thad."

"I'm extraordinarily aware of how much of a damn fool I look like," said J.J. as he walked to the center of the room. "All right, team, let's solve the Mystery of Whatever the Hell Wallace P. Gross Wanted Us to Find Down Here. Valentine, c'mere."

"What's up?"

"Grab my waist."

"What?"

"Grab my waist," repeated J.J. "Wallace P. Gross wanted us to cut a rug so we're gonna cut a rug."

"What's that gonna do?"

"I don't know. There's probably pressure-sensitive plates that, when pressed in the right order, will reveal a hidden passageway or something that'll lead us to the treasure."

"And the murderer?"

"And the murderer," repeated J.J.

"See, Wallace P. Gross was a master of creating puzzles. Ain't that right, Trudi?"

"Right," Trudi said absentmindedly. She was off searching in another part of the room.

J.J. wrapped his arms around his brother in an awkward embrace and began swaying slowly back and forth. "There's certain rules you play by when you're creating puzzles. First, you have to give the player a goal that they have to achieve." He twirled Valentine and pulled him into a tango, leading him around the room. "Then you have to give the player tools to achieve that goal," he said, dipping his very uncomfortable-looking brother and bringing him back upright.

Then, leaving his brother to do a little solo, free-form work, J.J. shimmied back toward the center of the room. "So in our case, the goal is whatever Wallace left for us in here and the tools provided to us are our slick, show-stopping dance moves."

Arriving in the center of the room, he did a couple of high kicks and then worked his way into a tried and true windmill spin. He transitioned that into a classic b-boy freeze, resting with his hands on the floor and his legs in the air. "Do you think we should try the Cha Cha Slide?" he asked, out of breath.

"Guys come over here, I think I've figured it out," Trudi said from the other end of the room.

J.J. broke his freeze and he and Val rushed over to where Trudi was crouching by a stack of chairs. She was staring at the floor.

"What is it?" asked Valentine.

"Doesn't this piece of carpet look strange to you?" she said, pointing down at the floor.

Examining the carpet closer, the brothers noticed there was a small, square patch that was a slightly different hue of red than the rest of the floor. It was held in place by several loose stitches.

"Wallace P. Gross's mysteries were almost always about saying one thing but meaning another," said Trudi. "What if by telling you guys to cut a rug, he actually, literally meant to cut open a rug?"

"It's worth a shot," said J.J. "Once I start doing the Cupid Shuffle I've officially run out of ideas." He reached into his satchel and produced a Ghost Hunters Adventure Club-branded plastic letter opener. "The idea was to pass these out and if, hypothetically, you were sent a ransom letter made out of pasted-together magazine clippings, you'd be opening it with a novelty gift that had our logo on it." He wedged the letter opener in between the stitchings and began cutting. Before long he had extricated the square patch, revealing a bare patch of concrete.

"Load of good that did," he said.

"Hold on a second," Trudi interrupted. She reached into the carpet through the hole that they had created and felt around under it. Probing with her fingers, she soon grabbed hold of something. She pulled her hand out, revealing a small piece of paper that looked like this:

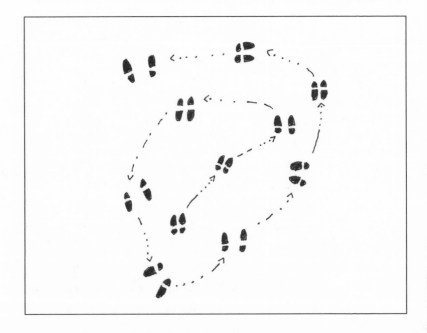

"What's that?" asked Valentine.

Trudi held it to the light and turned it around in her hand. "I think it's dance notation. The steps might correspond to a sequence of dance moves, but I don't know how this is gonna help us."

"Oh, that's easy," said J.J. as he grabbed the card and walked to the center of the ballroom. "Remember what I said about puzzles needing tools to be solved? Turns out I was right all along. I just didn't have the right dance steps."

J.J. stood under the chandelier and pointed himself toward the entrance to the ballroom. "These steps don't say where to start, so I'm going to orientate myself toward the door, since as long as I've known Wallace P. Gross he had an affinity for opening and closing doors. Valentine, may I have this dance?"

Valentine sighed and joined his brother at the center of the ballroom, giving him his hand. J.J. wrapped one arm around his brother and placed his other hand, holding the dance card, over his shoulder so that he could still reference it.

"Couple steps this way…over to here…then we twirl around in a circle and we end up…here." J.J. looked at his brother. "You feel any pressure-sensitive plates while we were dancing?"

Valentine shook his head.

"Right, then it has to be something else." He thought for a moment, making sure to maintain his correct position in the ballroom. "I've got it!" he exclaimed.

J.J. drew a direct line with his hands toward the wall he was facing, then walked directly toward that wall. "Wallace P. Gross, you sneaky snake," he said. "If my suspicions are correct, then this…" he said, grasping the electric candelabra in front of him, "is where we need to go next."

With all his might he pulled down on the lighting fixture. At first, a crack formed along the edges where the brass met the wall, then the whole fixture came loose, pulling a chunk of drywall with it. The light hung by an electrical cord as dust settled around J.J.'s feet. "Maybe there's another note inside the wall," he said. Peeking in, he only found more electrical wiring and some insulation. He left the light hanging off of its cord and walked back to the center of the room.

"The bad news is that I've committed serious property damage. The good news is that every failed solution brings us that much closer to the correct answer. Here's what I'm thinking…" He walked to the center of the room and turned about face. "Maybe Wallace P. Gross was more countercultural than I thought. Maybe he shunned the idea of doorways." He neglected a partner this time and performed the dance steps in accordance with the card and ended his routine facing the opposite direction.

"Then we just walk over to this light over here and…" he gave it another hearty yank. "Presto!"

More drywall sprinkled onto the carpet. There was nothing of interest behind the wall.

"Two cardinal directions down, two to go."

J.J. ripped out two more lighting fixtures to no avail. He then figured he might be doing the dance wrong. He tested out the samba, the tango, and the foxtrot with the help of both Valentine and Trudi (when J.J. wasn't satisfied with Valentine's form and commitment), then moved on to a final quick try with new American free-form. Each new dance either placed J.J. in the same direction as before or pointed him toward a chair or table, neither of which provided any new clues.

"All right, I'm ready to begin systematically tearing out all of these lighting fixtures. Looks like they're solid brass so if worse comes to worst I know a guy in Harborville who'll give us a buck-twenty-eight per pound."

"Wait a second," said Trudi, "we have to be missing something."

"You're right," J.J. said. "How *can* we carry that much brass out of the chateau without anyone noticing? Is there a laundry cart we could use to take it out the back entrance?"

"No," said Trudi, "with the clue. Remember, it's always about saying one thing and meaning another. He was a master at hiding the truth in plain sight."

"You're right," said Valentine. "Let me see that dance card again."

J.J. handed the dance card over to his brother, who studied it intently.

"If it isn't the dance moves that are the solution," Valentine said, "and Wallace is known for hiding his clues in plain sight, then what are we left with?"

Valentine gasped. "I've got it!"

J.J. and Trudi crowded behind him. He pointed at the lines between the foot markers. "What do those dots and dashes look like to you?"

"That's Morse code!" J.J. fished out his own beaten-up copy of the Ghost Hunters Adventure Club Field Manual and flipped it over to the cryptography chapter. First he transcribed the dots and dashes into a margin of the book so that they looked like this:

-.... --... --... .-.-.- -.... ....- .-.. -.... -.... .....

Then he referenced each set of dots and dashes to the Morse code table he had made sure to include in the field guide.

"Remind me to schedule some time for us all to memorize Morse code. I feel like that could come in handy later down the road."

Once he had figured out each character, they were left with a message:

677.64L665

"Is it a phone number?" asked Valentine.

"It's two numbers too long for that and one number short if we're talking about area codes," replied J.J. "Plus 'L' is not a number."

"It's the Dewey decimal system!" exclaimed Trudi.

"How'd you figure that out?"

"I like reading books. The 600s are the technology classification."

"There's a library one door over," said Valentine.

J.J. brushed off a bit of drywall that was stuck to his red sweater. "Looks like we know where we're going next."

Valentine led the trio out of the ballroom and slowly peeked his head out of the door, peering left and right. "The coast is clear. Let's go."

They closed the ballroom doors behind them and scurried past the grand staircase. Valentine opened the door to the library, breathing a sigh of relief that no one else was in there. He entered, Trudi close behind him. J.J. arrived last.

It was upon closing the door, with just a sliver of light illuminating a portion of his face, that J.J. looked down into the lobby of the Grande Chateau. It was in that briefest of moments that he locked eyes with Deputy Park, strolling out of the restaurant while he worked his molars with a toothpick.

J.J. shut the door and put his back to it. "Guys, we have a problem."

"What is it?" asked Trudi.

"Code Park. We spent so much time trying to figure out the ballroom that he must've finished eating. I don't know if he recognized me but he looked suspicious. Also, he had the steak judging by the fact that he was using a toothpick. I don't know if that's relevant to the situation but I figured I should mention it." J.J. frantically scanned the room for ideas. The jump out the window would be cushioned by the snow pile below, but the broken window would cause more questions. Too risky. There was once a vantage point looking into the library from the secret passageway but that was too small and was now probably blocked off. No good. If he could find a way to string two books together he could create a nunchaku for self-defense, but Deputy Park had a gun. Too dangerous. "Unless he considers himself an honorable man, then he'd have to engage me in hand-to-hand combat."

"What was that?" asked Valentine.

"Nothing!" J.J. ran to the light switches on the wall and shut them off, plunging the room into darkness. "Find a place to hide!"

Valentine and Trudi both slid under some lengthy mahogany tables at one end of the room. On the opposite end, J.J. dove behind a shelf of books that created an island between another rack of books. The trio waited where they landed, frozen.

"J.J., what do we do?" Valentine whispered from across the room.

"First step is to keep hiding. I haven't figured out the next step yet, but I'm all ears if you have any suggestions."

Just then the doors to the library flung open. Deputy Park's body cast a long shadow along the darkened library. Trudi clasped her hands to her mouth and tried to slow her breathing. J.J. kept scanning his surroundings for any bright ideas, but so far "bookchaku" seemed like the only semi-reasonable option.

"Hey! Is anyone in here?" asked Deputy Park. The only response was silence. He flipped on his flashlight and began sweeping it across the room. Valentine had to inch his way further to the side to avoid being caught in the beam. "I'm an officer of the law, so legally you have to tell me if you're in here or else I'm allowed to engage you in hand-to-hand combat."

Nice! thought J.J., but he couldn't find any durable string to make the bookchaku and the crafting of it might create too much noise. Maybe he could push a bookshelf onto the officer and everyone could run out in the ensuing chaos. He wondered how many years in the clink he'd get for assaulting a police officer.

An idea flashed through Valentine's head. He had to get his brother's attention. Leaning over to get an eyeline, he hissed, "J.J.!"

Deputy Park's flashlight swung over to the source of the noise. "What was that?" Although he maintained the composure of Harborville Sheriff's Department's finest, an astute observer could catch a hint of fear in his voice.

What Valentine wanted to say, if the whole team wasn't in the predicament that they were in and a beam of light wasn't currently trained on him, was that he remembered something specific about Deputy Park; the last time they were in a bind like this, Deputy Park had spoken at length about ghosts—arguably more than a normal person would talk at length about ghosts. This led Valentine to believe that they could simply scare Deputy Park away. With ghosts.

But things being what they were, all he could do was make eye contact with J.J. and mouth the words "SU-PER-STITIOUS."

J.J. stared at his brother with a blank expression. "I don't know how soup and dishes are gonna help," he whispered.

The flashlight swung across the room toward the bookshelf that J.J. was hiding behind. "Who's there?" There was a crack in Deputy Park's voice.

With the flashlight beam off of him, Valentine summoned the courage to speak again. "He's superstitious," he said in the loudest voice that could still be considered a whisper.

A look of realization washed over J.J.'s face as the flashlight swung away from him. He could hear the officer's heavy breathing from all the way over on his side of the room. Slowly he got up, hugging close to the shelf of books in front of him. Using his pointer finger, he poked a book off of the shelf with all his might. It flew through the air and landed face down on the floor with a thud.

Deputy Park's knees locked. His flashlight immediately trained on the book on the floor. By matter of pure luck, J.J. was in the paranormal research section of the library and the book was *How to Hunt Ghosts* by Joshua P. Warren.

Seeing his success with the first book, J.J. felt it was appropriate to raise the stakes. He dipped down to a lower portion of the book shelf and let a couple more volumes fly. They landed scattered on the floor of the library, their pages splayed open.

Deputy Park remained in place, paralyzed by fear. He trembled, searching for words to say but not summoning enough courage to say them.

Time for the big guns, J.J. thought. He slid away from the bookshelf to get as close to the deputy as possible. In the scratchiest, most unsettling voice he could muster, he hissed, "LEEEEEAVE."

Deputy Park stiffened like a plank. He spoke in a monotone voice. "There are forces in play here that exist past the veil of human comprehension. Good day, spirits."

With that, the deputy turned around and left the library, slamming the door behind him.

The trio waited for some time to make sure Deputy Park was gone before they all collapsed to the floor and caught their breath. J.J. was the first to get up. "The classic spooky bookcase trick. Good thinking, Val. Remind me of that the next time we do your annual performance review."

"Let's just find the book and get out of here," said Valentine. "Trudi, where are the 600s?"

Trudi got out from under the table and went over to the bookshelf that J.J. had been hiding near. She began thumbing through book spines, counting as she went. "610...640..."

She moved over to an adjacent bookshelf and continued searching. "Here it is!"

J.J. and Valentine crowded behind her as she located the book labeled 677.64L665. Pulling it out, she examined the cover. "*The Complete Carpet Manual* by Jerry Levinstein."

"Cute," said Valentine.

Flipping through the pages, Trudi stopped at the chapter discussing spot carpet repair. Between the pages was a single sheet of paper cut diagonally. On it were jumbled letters that made no sense to them. "I think this is the other half of the letter Marcella P. Gross received from her husband," said Trudi.

J.J. let out a heavy sigh. "Guys, I think I'm going to have to do the hardest thing I've ever done in my life."

"What's that?" asked Valentine.

"I'm going to have to sincerely apologize to someone."

CHAPTER 13

Sincerely Apologizing to Someone

J.J. paced outside of the door to Marcella P. Gross's suite, muttering under his breath everything that he had practiced with Valentine and Trudi about empathy and apologizing and basic human decency. There was a brief moment when he thought about running away from the suite, through the hallway, down the stairs, out the lobby doors, into the snow, and to the nearest traveling circus he could find to start life anew as a carnival barker, but most traveling circuses went south for the winter. What if he became a longshoreman? He'd get to grow a beard…

J.J. shook those thoughts from his head. "You can do this," he said to himself with a vulnerability he reserved for when no one was listening.

Taking a deep breath, he knocked on Marcella's door. It was a moment before the door cracked open, revealing Marcella's face in a slit of light. J.J. could tell that she had been crying.

"What do you want?"

J.J. took the dumb fedora that he had nicked from the lost and found off of his head and placed it over his heart in a show of sincerity. He figured props would help him in his most dire hour of need. "Ma'am, I'd like to wholeheartedly and without reservation apologize for my actions earlier today, I—"

Marcella slammed the door in his face.

J.J. took a moment to collect himself, then calmly knocked on the door once more. She cracked the door open.

"What?"

Hat on heart, look a little teary-eyed, take a deep breath.

"I just want to say I'm sorry for—"

She slammed the door in his face again.

J.J. felt his temper rising and fought his natural urge to scream well-crafted obscenities. He counted to ten, as his brother had instructed him to do, then leaned in close to the door.

"Okay, if you don't want to do this face-to-face I'll say it through the door. What I did today was way out of line. I accused you without any real evidence, and embarrassed you in front of your peers. It was because of my own bullheadedness that I put you in this position. And for that, I'm truly sorry."

He listened to the door for what felt to him like forever. Then he heard Marcella's voice.

"You can take your apology and stuff it up your nose, Jack."

It was right about here that J.J. lost his temper. Adrenaline pumped through his veins and he only saw red. "Listen here, you old bird! I come here with a literal hat in hand to make nice and you insult me! I hope you're happy with Thad Newbury and his stupid ponytail!"

"If you really wanted to apologize to me you could go build a time machine and stop yourself from prying into my private life! Better yet, you should probably stop yourself from being born, you little street urchin!"

"Yeah? Well if I had a time machine, first I'd give myself a sports almanac from the future so that I could make my millions off of gambling, then I'd watch the Hindenburg crash because that's an interesting piece of history I'd like to experience firsthand, *then* I'd travel back to the time of the dinosaurs so I could challenge you to a fair fight in your physical prime!"

"You couldn't handle me today!" Marcella's voice shrieked through the door. "I'd rip your throat out, watch you die, then wait patiently until I died happily of old age so I could kill you again in the afterlife!"

"Oh, come at me, you blood-sucking vampire! I will bury you and the whole town will celebrate my valiance once I've freed them from the darkness that's beset them for centuries!"

Just then, Marcella swung the door open, huffing and puffing, glaring at J.J. despite her small and frail stature. He steeled his nerves and puffed out his chest, ready for a fight he had asked for but questioning his own threat to punch an old lady.

It was only a moment before her features softened. The rage left her eyes and she spoke in as kind of a tone as a battle-hardened spinster could. "You're all right, kid. Come on in." She stood beside the doorway and motioned for J.J. to enter. He moved forward warily, checking the floor for any sort of booby trap. Stepping into the suite, J.J. noticed that it was much better decorated than any other suite he had seen in the Grande Chateau. Victorian silhouettes hung on the walls and a red shawl lay draped over the only source of light, casting the room in crimson.

"I travel with my own picture frames," she explained. "It helps me feel grounded."

She offered up an easy chair in the corner of the room and asked, "Tea?"

"Sure," said J.J., his mind racing with thoughts about the poison she must be putting into it to finish him once and for all.

"You know, you remind me a lot of how Wallace used to be when he was younger," she said, pouring hot water from a kettle into two teacups. "Hard-nosed, defiant, quick to come to conclusions…"

She handed him a tea cup and saucer. J.J. eyed it warily.

"Oh calm down, it's not poisoned. If I wanted to kill you I'd have shot you with the crossbow I keep under my bed."

"You keep a crossbow under your bed?"

"Wouldn't you like to know? So what brings you here, gumshoe? I know you're not the type of gentleman to apologize without motive."

J.J. took a sip of the tea and immediately spat it back into the cup. "This is mostly vodka."

Marcella shrugged.

"It's about the letter you received from Wallace before he died," he said, placing the teacup and saucer on a coffee table in front of him. "I think we might have found the other half."

Marcella raised her eyebrows. "Did you now. What did it say?"

"It was all gibberish, ma'am. I was hoping that by combining the two, you and I could make some sense out of it."

"That's just like Wallace to do," said Marcella. "Always with his little games. Come on, let's try and figure it out."

J.J. pulled the diagonally-cut piece of paper the team had found in the library from his satchel and handed it to Marcella, who sat down at her desk and produced her half from one of the drawers. J.J. got up and looked over her shoulder.

Combining the two sheets of paper into one, it now looked like this:

```
              Q C    W A I I X L I E V X ,
              M J    C S Y ' V I   V I E H M R K
   X L M W    X L I R   M ' Z I   Q I X   Q C   J E X I .
              M   W S P Z I H   X L I   Q C W X I V C .
     N S L R   K V E R H I ' W   J S V X Y R I .
   X M Q I   M W   W L S V X   E R H   M ' Q
 Y R H I V   W Y V Z I M P P E R G I .   M   P I J X
        X L I   M R J S V Q E X M S R
           G S R G I E P I H   M R   Q C   R I A
     F S S O   A L M G L   M ' Z I   L M H H I R
       X S   F I   J S Y R H .   Q E V G I P P E ,
     R I Z I V   J S V K I X   Q C   P S Z I   J S V
 C S Y .   I Z I R   R S A   M   G E R ' X   F I
   G L E J I H   E F S Y X   X L E H .   L I
 A M P P   X V I E X   C S Y   F I X X I V
   X L E R   M   I Z I V   G S Y P H .
   Q E C   X L I   V I W X   S J   C S Y V
   P M J I   F I   O M R H   X S   C S Y .
```

Beware the monster
at the end of the maze

"Well that doesn't help," said J.J. "It's all still gibberish."

Marcella scoffed. "That's because it's written in code. Pull up a chair, young man. You might learn something valuable here."

J.J. dragged his chair over while Marcella continued to speak. "Wallace was obsessed with puzzles. It was his idea of courtship to leave multi-part cryptograms for me to solve. It bled into his writing and next thing you know, you have an international bestselling author who doesn't make time for his wife."

"If it's written in code, wouldn't we need a key of some sort to solve it?"

"Sweet child, Wallace hasn't given me a decoding key since our third date. If this is as simple as a substitution code, we can figure it out in minutes. What's the most frequently occurring letter in the English language?"

"D," said J.J. as quickly as he could.

"Did you just say the first letter that you could think of off the top of your head?"

"It was a one in twenty-six chance. I liked the odds."

"The most used letter in the English language is 'E.' So if a coded message is long enough, a good place to start is to find the most frequently used letter in the message and see if it's in places where 'E' is commonly used."

They scanned over the combined piece of paper letter for letter.

"The letter 'I' shows up a lot, doesn't it?" said J.J.

"Points for the newbie. Now, since this message contains apostrophes, that makes it even easier." She pointed at "C S Y ' V I" in the second line and "M ' Z I" in the third. "How many contractions can you think of that use two letters that don't have the letter 'E' in them?"

J.J. thought for a moment, giving this question an earnest effort for once. "There's 'you'll.'"

"And not much else," said Marcella. "So unless this is a shifting cipher, where the code changes for every letter or word—and we'd need a supercomputer to solve it anytime this century—we can assume that these words might be a contraction: 'HOW'VE, 'YOU'RE,' or 'I'VE.' Are you still following me?"

"Best as I can, ma'am."

"Good. Now there's two types of ciphers that are very commonly used, the Caesar cipher and the Atbash cipher. A Caesar cipher is where you find your code word by shifting the alphabet forward or backward a certain amount of letters. An Atbash cipher is where you mirror the alphabet on top of itself, so that 'A' translates to 'Z,' 'B' translates to 'Y,' and so forth."

"So which one is this?" asked J.J.

"Use your head, youngster. You tell me."

J.J. furrowed his brows and studied the 'I's in the message. "The letter 'E' is pretty close to the letter 'I,' so for right now I think we can rule out the Atbash cipher."

"Good observation."

"Then the letter 'E' is four letters away from the letter 'I,' so what if this was a Caesar cipher and the shift is four?"

"There's hope for you yet. So how can you test this out?"

J.J. ripped a piece of paper from the complimentary Grande Chateau-branded stationery in Marcella's suite and copied down "W A I I X L I E V X" from the first line of the message. After a bit of mental math, J.J. translated the word.

"Sweetheart," he said.

"Congratulations," said Marcella. "You figured out the key."

"Holy moly, I'm a master sleuth."

"Don't develop an ego, kid. This is literally one of the easiest crypto-grams to solve."

Marcella took another piece of stationery and placed it next to the two divided sheets of paper that Wallace had left them. With remarkable speed she translated each letter of the coded message. In a little over a minute she had completed the puzzle. Her piece of stationery now read:

> My sweetheart,
> if you're reading
> this then I've met my fate.
> I solved the mystery.
> John Grande's fortune.
> Time is short and I'm
> Under surveillance. I left
> The information
> concealed in my new
> book which I've hidden
> To be found. Marcella,
> never forget my love for
> you. Even now I can't be
> Chafed about Thad. He
> Will treat you better
> than I ever could.
> May the rest of your
> life be kind to you.

Marcella sat in silence, reading and rereading the newly decoded message. J.J. knew better than to interrupt her.

"He…knew he was going to die," she said. "And he knew about Thad. Although I'm less impressed about that. Thad has a big mouth."

"I'm, uh, sorry for your loss, ma'am. It seems like Wallace really cared about you up until the end."

"He did. He was horrible to be married to, but he did care. Imagine having to solve twenty years' worth of these types of puzzles on a daily basis. Sure, it's a cute thing to do for a proposal, but the bit grows old when you're holding a piece of paper up to a mirror to figure out what you have to get from the grocery store."

J.J. stared at the original coded piece of paper. "This can't be it, though."

"What do you mean?"

"I'm, uh…glad you got some closure out of the recent events, but that means me and my team—"

"My team and I."

"Right, that means my team and I are at a dead end. We were finding and solving clues up until this point, but if this is all there is to it, then I have no idea where to go next."

Marcella smirked. "That's just like Wallace to do. To say one thing and then hide the true meaning within it. Let's look at that puzzle again."

They stared at the original puzzle, searching for something they may have missed.

J.J. pointed at the handwritten note at the bottom of the page. "'Beware the monster at the end of the maze.' We saw that down in the secret passage, too. Could that phrase have something to do with solving the mystery?"

"It could. It's absolutely Wallace's handwriting. But I'm not sure what we can glean from that. Additionally, it was on the sheet of paper that was delivered to me, not the one you found."

"Hmm…We have to be missing something."

He stared at the original coded message for a long time, searching for any hints that might lead them to a solution. Frustrated, he turned his attention over to the decrypted message, reading and rereading it over and over again. "Wait, look here," he said, pointing at the decrypted message. "Wallace used the word 'chafed' when he was speaking about Thad. Don't you think that's an odd choice? He could have just as easily used the word 'mad' or 'angry,' and it would have had a better effect."

"Maybe he used that word because he had to use it to fit into a code."

"Right, and look here." J.J. pointed at the margins of the page of the original encrypted document. "Each line of the puzzle has a different indentation. Maybe he was trying to line up letters so that they could spell something out."

Marcella laughed, "You know, kid, you're smarter than your words and actions and everything you've done since I've met you have let on."

"Thanks, I think. But what was he trying to say and where can we find it?"

"Remember that Wallace does everything deliberately," Marcella said. "By this point he's created enough puzzles to fill an entire encyclopedia set. He knows what he's doing."

J.J. kept scanning the original puzzle for any sort of intentional inaccuracy that might go along with the odd indentations. First he tried counting the spaces before each line started and applying those numbers to their corresponding letters in the line, but that turned up nothing. Then he tried counting the periods and apostrophes in the hope it was hidden Morse code like the last puzzle. Still nothing.

Then, a flash.

"I've got it!" J.J. shouted.

"Well, then, what's the solution, kid?"

J.J. pointed at the puzzle where it had been cut in two. "Do you see how this diagonal line split the paper? It's not splitting it in half, as you might have expected Wallace to do. Instead it cuts directly through a line of letters. So if you follow the line on the piece of paper that was meant for my team and I—"

"Me and my team. Learn your grammar, son. It's valuable."

"Right. If you follow the line on the letter that was meant for me and my team, then you get this set of letters."

J.J. grabbed the pen and jotted the following onto a new sheet of paper:

A L I V I A I J M V W X Q I X

"Now what does that translate to?" asked J.J.

Marcella took the pen and made quick work of the code. Above the letters she wrote:

W H E R E W E F I R S T M E T

"Where we first met," said Marcella.

J.J. looked puzzled. "I don't know why Wallace would want us to go back to his study to look around. We've already combed that place for clues."

"Unless he meant where he and I first met."

J.J. jumped up, excited. "I remember this! He told us that you two met under the big angel statue where you were sitting on that bench just after you threatened his life and gave us reasonable concern to suspect you of murder!"

Marcella nodded. "That's the place."

J.J. put his dumb fedora back on and headed toward the door. "Are you coming? There's treasure at the end of this trail."

Marcella took a sip of her tea. "I've had enough adventure for one lifetime. I received the closure I needed from the letter. You go on ahead. Just beware of the monster at the end of the maze, I suppose."

J.J. opened the door to Marcella's suite, then turned around to address her one last time. "Thanks for the help, you vicious siren of the night."

Marcella smiled. "I will haunt your dreams."

J.J. closed the door behind him and stepped out into the hallway. He knew where the team had to go next and they were that much closer to John Henry Grande's fortune.

He had just gotten to the elevator when he was struck across the back of his head, knocking off his dumb fedora.

J.J. dropped to his knees, his vision blurring and fading around the edges. As he fell over and the world turned to black, the last thing he remembered was the sensation of being dragged along the carpet of the fourth floor of the Grande Chateau.

CHAPTER 14

Man Down

Valentine checked his watch repeatedly while he paced around their room which felt smaller and smaller by the moment. There was nothing good on TV and the view out of the window provided the exact same scenery as the last time he checked.

"It's been an hour," he said.

"What'd J.J. say to do when it's been an hour?" asked Trudi. She was lying down on one of the beds, rereading a Wallace P. Gross mystery novel.

"He said to abort the mission and disavow any knowledge of his existence until five calendar years have passed. At that point he demands that we begin telling stories of his heroic life, making sure to embellish the stories in different ways each time so that he could live on as a great American tall tale."

"Right." She dog eared the book and sat on the edge of the bed, watching Valentine pace. "I mean, what could have happened to him between here and Marcella's room?"

"Deputy Park could have caught him. The real killer could've taken him out when he was alone and unaware. Marcella could have ground his teenager bones into her soup for all we know."

"We should go looking for him," said Trudi.

"What if he really had to work his magic with Marcella and he's just now finally getting the next clue? He could be in there right now, and you know how he is about sincere apologies."

"Marcella's suite is the first place we can check. If he's not there we can look around the chateau. We're surrounded by snow. How far could he have gotten?"

* * *

THE WORLD SLOWLY CAME BACK into focus for J.J., who could tell he had been drooling on himself. He tried to massage the dull ache in the back of his head but found his arms were tied behind his back. His legs didn't fare much better: they were bound to the legs of the chair he was sitting in. Attempting to speak, he found his mouth was bound as well.

The handkerchief was soaked in drool.

J.J. fought the urge to panic. His Ghost Hunters Adventure Club training had prepared him for the unlikely event he was incapacitated by an unknown assailant and woke up bound and gagged in a foreign environment. He had devoted an entire chapter to it in the field manual.

It was cold, wherever he was. The drool had formed into frost on certain parts of his sweater. He was losing feeling in his extremities.

The lone source of light in the room was a lamp hanging from the ceiling by a cord, swaying slightly and casting harsh shadows along the wall. Looking around the room, he cased his surroundings. He was in a room with sheet metal walls. There was a small ventilation window on one of the walls near the ceiling, but it was impossible to reach. Hanging on the wall in front of him was a gigantic saw. Below it was a workbench filled with a variety of fear-inducing power drills, augers, ice picks, band saws, vice grips, and...

His heart leapt. His satchel hung on the wall among the tools. It was out of reach for him, his being tied to the chair and all. He would have to find a way to get to it.

Lying in the far corner was the frozen body of Wallace P. Gross, propped in a sitting position against the wall. J.J. fought back another gasp, seeing his own grisly fate in the exploded head of the now-dead author.

I've seen enough true crime documentaries to know when I'm in a kill room, he thought, quickly shooing the words from his mind. *I couldn't have been out for long so I must not have gone very far. There's still hope for me. This'll make for a great chapter in my eventual memoir: "Ghost Hunting, Crime Solving, and Impossibly Good Looks: The Story of J.J. Watts, as Written by J.J. Watts, Because He Didn't Die in a Scary Kill Room."*

It was cold and the wind was howling, so he decided he must not be in the chateau anymore. But if he wasn't there, then where was he?

And then he saw it: his potential escape plan. Next to the work bench with all the scary tools, hanging at eye level to J.J. seated and bound to his chair, was a telephone.

It was Grande Chateau-branded. He must still be somewhere on the property!

J.J. wriggled his neck back and forth in an attempt to dislodge the handkerchief gag around his neck. He pushed out with his tongue and worked in conjunction with his teeth. With great effort and vigorous movements with his head, he was finally able to bring the handkerchief down to his chin. One more shake of the neck and the soggy, drool-soaked gag hung down around his neck.

Now free of the first binding—but with many more to go—J.J. was finally able to speak.

"Shit."

* * *

VALENTINE AND TRUDI WALKED UPSTAIRS together toward the top floor of the Grande Chateau. A worried expression seemed permanently stuck on Valentine's face.

"What if we run into Deputy Park?" asked Trudi.

"We tell him the truth. J.J. is missing and we don't know what happened to him. I'm not gonna lose my own brother just to find some treasure."

"Are you actually brothers?" asked Trudi at the top of the stairwell.

Valentine stopped at the door to the fourth floor and turned to look Trudi directly in her eyes. "I'm contractually unable to answer that question."

They walked down the hallway to Marcella's door.

Valentine took a deep breath and raised his hand to knock, pulling away at the last second. "What if she grinds *our* teenager bones into her soup?"

"Just knock on the door already."

Valentine knocked on the door and the two waited. After a moment the door swung open to reveal Marcella P. Gross. She rolled her eyes when she saw them.

"Oh come on, I'm not gonna help you solve any more clues. I'm not running a charity here."

"Ms. Gross," Valentine said, "we were just wondering if you know what happened to—"

Marcella slammed the door in their faces.

"—my brother, because we can't find him."

Valentine tried knocking again but Marcella didn't bother with coming back. Dejected, he and Trudi walked back down the hallway toward the elevator.

"I don't get it," said Valentine. "What could have happened between him leaving Marcella's room and coming back to our room?"

"What about Deputy Park?"

"I've personally witnessed J.J. talk himself out of tougher predicaments with officers of the law. I don't think a chance run-in alone with Park would have been that difficult for him."

Arriving at the elevator, Trudi was the first to see J.J.'s dumb fedora lying on the floor. Picking it up, she offered it to Valentine.

"This was J.J.'s wasn't it?"

"It was. And I know he'd never be the sort of person to leave a dumb fedora lying on the floor, especially when he said he needed something to do with his hands while he apologized to Marcella."

Valentine turned the dumb fedora around in his hand, examining it. "Something bad's happened to J.J., and we need to find him. Quick."

* * *

J.J. APPROXIMATED THE DISTANCE between himself and the phone at the far end of the wall. Ten feet. He had fidgeted for a while with the rope bindings on his wrist and had tried kicking himself out of the knot that his legs were tied with, but nothing loosened the grip. He would have to find another way to get there. Another way to dial the numbers. Another way to contact help.

He figured he'd do it the old fashioned way. Summoning all of his strength, he lurched his body forward and pushed off of the ground with his feet. The maneuver worked, and the chair took a short hop forward.

That's one.

J.J. had no idea when whoever had put him here would come back, so he had to work fast. He repeated the lurching, kicking motion again and again, bringing him inches closer to the telephone each time. Another lurch, another kick, another few inches.

Beads of sweat formed on his forehead despite the coldness of the room. He took a small break to measure his progress.

A solid two feet. Cool.

J.J. knew he had to speed this up, or else he'd never get out of here in time. With a mighty push forward, he launched himself up into the air along with the chair. The J.J. Watts Space Program in full effect. Landing on the ground a full foot forward, he could feel that his body had shifted in the launch, turning his rightmost chair legs toward the telephone. The momentum of the shift carried him forward. The chair teetered onto those two legs and his center of gravity shifted. He was about to fall onto his side!

Course correct! Course correct! the tiny versions of J.J. scrambling inside the imagined mission control center in his head warned. J.J. gasped and hurled his body weight in the opposite direction. Swinging back in the other way, J.J.'s chair landed on all fours. There was a brief moment of relief before his eyes widened as he began teetering in the opposite direction.

Course correct again! the tiny J.J.s begged. *But maybe not as much this time!*

J.J. hurled himself again, pushing his center of gravity back over. He heaved a great sigh of relief as all four of his chair legs touched the ground and stayed there.

"Okay, okay, baby steps it is," said J.J.

He went back to the tried and true lurch-and-push method, first to get him facing the telephone, then to continue the inch-by-inch crawl toward freedom. He managed to close the last seven feet without incident in a little under thirty minutes.

Drenched in sweat and shivering because of it, J.J. formed his plan of attack. With a great sweep of his face, he managed to knock the receiver off of its base, landing on the work bench to his right. The coiled cord remained attached to both the receiver and base, and from the ear phone he could hear a dial tone.

"Score one for me."

Next, and with great precision, he began pecking at the numbers on the base of the phone with his nose. One by one, he nosed each number until he had completed the seven to make a call, then leaned his head over to the receiver on the workbench.

The telephone in his and Valentine's suite that J.J. had secured for himself and his brother rang unanswered twenty times before J.J. gave up.

* * *

VALENTINE AND TRUDI ELECTED TO TAKE the elevator down to the lobby of the Grande Chateau.

"Let's see if we can blend in with the crowd," Valentine suggested. "Maybe J.J.'s down there trying to pull a quick grift before he came upstairs."

"Yeah, but if Madame Fournier or Deputy Park catch us looking suspicious, we're toast."

"It's well past midnight, so I assume Fournier is out for the night, but you're right about Park. Let's keep our eyes peeled."

The doors to the elevator opened and they jumped back in fright—there was someone standing right in front of them. They both breathed a sigh of relief once they realized it wasn't Deputy Park. Valentine recognized the woman as the bartender of the Grande Chateau.

"Yo! Trudi!" she said in a thick Bostonian accent. "Heard you got canned."

"Yeah, Carolina, it blows."

"It's a shame. You were a real inspiration to all of us who wanted to look like we were working while doing the least amount of work possible. I'm gonna miss ya."

"Me too," said Trudi.

She and Valentine exited the elevator and Carolina took their place.

"The new guy sucks too."

"What? I already got replaced?"

"Yeah, he's a lot like you in that he doesn't care about his job, but nothing like you in that it's not in a fun way. Welp, happy trails."

The door to the elevators closed and they walked down the grand staircase to the lobby where, even at midnight, a few hotel patrons were milling around. Valentine scanned the crowd.

No J.J.

Trudi looked across the lobby to spot a pockmarked teenager with shaggy hair in a Grande Chateau uniform at the front desk. From this far away she didn't even need her powers of deduction to tell that he was an idiot.

"Aw man, they really did replace me."

Valentine spotted the danger first. Leaving the restaurant with a newspaper rolled under his arm was none other than Deputy Park.

"We gotta jam," Valentine hissed. He grabbed Trudi by the hand and pulled her to the side. They dove behind the empty bar, crouching on top of a rubber slip mat, surrounded by drink mixes and liquor bottles.

"We should be safe here, right?" asked Valentine.

"Carolina's the only bartender and she already went to her room for the night. We can stay here for as long as we need to."

Officer Park sat down at one of the barstools in front of the bar and unfurled his newspaper, engrossing himself in days-old news. Without looking up, he said, "Carolina, there's nothing more I need in this world right now than a whiskey sour."

* * *

WITH GREAT EFFORT AND ABOVE-AVERAGE FLEXIBILITY, J.J. managed to catch the switch hook with his nose and hold it down for long enough to end the call and get a new dial tone. He searched his brain for any number he could call.

Dialing eleven numbers this time, he leaned over to the handset and heard an odd dial tone. It took him a minute to realize that this was a closed telephone line. You had to dial "9" to get out.

Once again catching the switch hook with his nose but swearing a lot more this time, J.J. heard the dial tone, made sure to press "9" first so that he could make an outside call, then pressed the same eleven numbers with his nose.

* * *

HOLD ON, MY PHONE'S RINGING.

I walk over to the kitchen in my cabin and pick up the handset, hook my fingers into the base, and bring it over to the kitchen table. Settling down comfortably, I answer.

"Hello?"

"Doc! Doc, things are pretty bad."

"Oh, hey J.J., you caught me in the middle of writing. What are you calling me about?"

"You sure as Susie know what I'm calling you about. I'm strapped to a chair in a kill room!"

"Whoa whoa whoa, slow down, kid. First of all, it's not a kill room and I resent that you'd call it that. This is a teen novel, after all."

J.J. did a little more swearing that I'd rather not write down here for fear of losing my publishing deal, but just know that his comments were unkind and hurtful.

As soon as he calmed down, he changed to a pleading tone. "Come on, Doc, gimme something to go off of here. This is all pretty dire."

"Absolutely not. That's the problem with you kids these days. Always looking for handouts. I'm not running a charity here."

"You already used that line when Valentine and Trudi spoke to Marcella."

"You're not supposed to know that, since you weren't in the scene when that took place."

There were a couple more profanities here.

"I'm sorry, son. You're just going to have to call someone else."

I hang up the phone to desperate protestations and sit back down to write. This book isn't going to finish itself, despite how badly I want it to.

* * *

TRUDI KNOCKED AGAINST some of the liquor bottles stored next to them. She looked to Valentine for help, who looked just as lost as she was. "You got it, Park," she said.

"What are you doing?" Valentine whisper-hissed.

"I don't know. I panicked, so I responded."

"Not that! You know Carolina has a Boston accent. Short O's and no R's. 'I pahk'd the cah in Ha'vahd yahd.' Keep him busy and I'll make the drink." He immediately began searching the storage shelf for a good rye whiskey.

"Everything okay over there?" asked Deputy Park. He remained nose-deep in his newspaper.

"It's frickin' fine back heah," said Trudi. She shot a glance at Valentine. "Do you even know how to make a whiskey sour?"

"I did a lot of things before I became a private eye and lying about my age to bartend may have been one of them," he said. "They don't have a pre-mix so I'm gonna have to squeeze some lemon juice. Could you hand me that simple syrup?"

"You know, Carolina," said Deputy Park, still transfixed on his reading, "this cop business can be too much for one man to handle sometimes."

"I heah ya. What's on yah mind, coppah?"

Deputy Park gave a resigned sigh. "Sometimes I wonder if there's more to this world than we think we know. Do you believe in the paranormal?"

"Like frickin' ghosts and whatnot?" Trudi turned to Valentine and shrugged.

Valentine leaned over to Trudi and whispered "Less Southie, add some upper class townie to it," he said as he cracked an egg and separated the whites into a metal shaker.

"What are you doing?" whispered Trudi.

"It creates a good froth. Nice mouth feel. Just keep him talking a little while longer."

"It's just…" Deputy Park gulped, "I was up in the library a bit ago thinking I saw something when a chill runs through my spine. I'm standing there, wondering if I had walked through a cold spot for a reason, when all of these books start flying off the shelves."

"Aw, yeah," said Trudi, "this spot's more haunted than Fenway. Rest in peace, Teddy Williams."

"Rest in peace," Deputy Park nodded. "I just don't know what I'm doing with my life when I'm not even sure what happens to you after you die."

"Me, I think what happens when yah die is that yah go up to tha big three-deckah in the sky, and all yah boys are there, and yah gramps is grilling…" Trudi paused. *What do Bostonians grill?* "…chowda. He's grillin' chowda in the backyahd." Trudi smacked her head.

"Boy, grilled chowder sounds amazing right about now," said Deputy Park. He turned the page in the newspaper. "I guess this spooky stuff is getting to me. Those Watts boys probably got it stuck in my head with their ghost hunting nonsense. They're not bad kids, you know. Just misguided."

Valentine smiled as he popped the metal containers together and gave it a good shake. He strained it out into a glass and garnished it with an orange slice and a cherry on a toothpick. Handing it over to Trudi, she reached up and no-look slid it to the sheriff's deputy.

"Here's looking at you, pal."

"Thanks, Care," he said as he no-look reached for his drink. "What do I owe you?"

"It's on tha house, Mack. You work too hahd."

"You're a sweetheart, Carolina." He took a sip and raised his eyebrows. "Carolina, this is the best damn whiskey sour I've ever had in my li—"

The blood drained from his face when he looked across the bar to find no one there.

* * *

RUSTY TIBBITS WAS AN IDIOT. Worse yet, he was an idiot with a job. At the age of sixteen he was dragged by his parents up to the Grande Chateau for a ski weekend that turned out to be the most boring weekend of his life—snowed in and stuck with his parents playing gin rummy. He spent the first day, when that strange writer was murdered, running around the chateau grounds looking for kids to bully. When he got tired of that, he watched reruns of daytime talk shows until his eyes bled. By the next day he was ready to walk out into the snow and take his chances down the mountain.

He couldn't stand his parents, couldn't stand his peers, and he couldn't understand those strange detective guys who kept messing everything up for people. If only he brought his videogame console, then maybe this weekend wouldn't have been so bad.

Rusty was in the crowd when that J.J. fella started yelling about murderers. He walked up the grand staircase to the study with the throngs of people and tried as best as he could to hear what that guy was screaming about, but he was standing in the back so all he could make out was that the guy made an old lady cry.

For some reason, the lady who managed the place came up to him after it. Madame Fore-Near or something like that.

"You look bored, young man," she said.

"I *am* bored."

"Splendid. I just had a job open up as the front desk receptionist. Do you have any experience in the position?"

"No," was his honest and unelaborated answer.

She looked a little cross, but pressed onward. "Are you interested at all in the world of hospitality management? It's a lucrative career path and you get to meet so many interesting people."

"Not really. I was kind of just here to ski but we can't do that right now."

"All right, well, can you just sit at a desk and answer a phone in exchange for money until the snow is cleared and I can hire someone new?"

Rusty thought for longer than it should have taken a reasonable person to answer this question. "Um, sure."

"Lovely!" said Madame Fournier. "Welcome to the team!"

It was after that conversation, and a fifteen minute training session that he half-listened to, that Rusty found himself where he had currently been sitting for the last several hours: the front desk reception area of the Grande Chateau. He spent most of this time doodling elaborate penises on the provided Grande Chateau-branded stationery.

It had been a relatively slow day, as far as Rusty knew. Nobody had stopped by to check in or check out on account of the snowstorm, but the computer in front of him did have solitaire. He gave up on it after one try.

And so it was that Rusty Tibbits was busying himself with people-watching late at night when a phone call came in, something he was neither trained in dealing with nor interested in learning. He picked up the phone.

"Grande Chateau."

"Oh thank Christmas, I've finally reached someone," said the voice on the other end of the line. "Listen, I've been kidnapped and I'm trapped somewhere I'm not familiar with. All I know is that it's somewhere on the Grande Chateau grounds because I'm using your phone right now."

Whatever they had trained Rusty in, it was definitely not this. "I'm sorry to hear that, sir. How may I assist you?"

"Okay, take a pen and notepad out because it's gonna be complicated. I'm gonna need you to—did you get the pen and notepad?"

"It's right beside me, sir."

"Okay, I need you to track down Valentine Watts and Trudi de la Rosa. They're supposed to be in room 337 but I called and no one answered. Valentine's a moderately handsome guy, but not too handsome. He's wearing a powder blue sweater and has glasses. As for Trudi, I think you used to work with her. Dark hair and glasses. Has a know-it-all attitude. Real delight at parties.

"Once you find them, I need you to tell them exactly what I told you: that I was kidnapped and I'm trapped somewhere around the chateau. It's cold and I can hear the wind outside so I don't think I'm attached to the building, if that helps. They'll be smart enough to figure out where it is and save me. Did you get all that?"

"Every word of it, sir," said Rusty Tibbits. He looked down at his notepad to admire the elaborately drawn penis he had just crafted. This one was maybe his best yet.

"Thanks, pal, you're a lifesaver."

Rusty finally remembered the one bit of training that he had paid attention to earlier in the day: be courteous. "No, sir, thank you. Please enjoy the rest of your stay at the Grande Chateau and don't hesitate to call me if you have any questions, comments, or concerns."

He hung up the phone and started drawing another penis. Practice made perfect.

* * *

DEPUTY PARK SLOWLY LIFTED HIMSELF from his barstool and backed away from the bar. He tried forming words, but the best he could manage were bumbled consonants and teeth chattering. Making sure to keep his eyes on the bar, he made the cautious, mechanical turn toward the elevators by the grand staircase. Satisfied that he had disengaged with the spirits, he began his hurried walk to safety.

Looking up from the doodle he had just started, Rusty Tibbits saw Deputy Park walking away as if he had to go to the bathroom. "Hey, police guy, what should I do if someone calls up the chateau telling you he was kidnapped and woke up somewhere on the grounds where it's cold and he can hear the wind outside?"

From their crouched positions behind the bar, Valentine and Trudi overheard the conversation. Valentine managed to stop himself from gasping by holding his hands over his mouth.

"You tell them no one knows what happens when we die and to love your wife and children and family and friends while you can because who's to say you can see them once it's all over?" Deputy Park hurried to the elevator and breathed a sigh of relief as he ascended to his room.

Rusty Tibbits shrugged. "He didn't leave a callback number."

"That's gotta be J.J.!" Valentine said. "But where is there a place on the chateau grounds that isn't attached to the chateau itself?"

Trudi thought for a moment, running through her knowledge of the chateau as it had existed in warmer months when everything wasn't covered in snow. She snapped her fingers, "I've got it! He must be in the storage shed. It's out in the back by the courtyard. We store all of the tools out there."

"We better hurry. We don't know how much time J.J. has left."

They waited until they were certain Deputy Park was no longer in the lobby before peeking their heads out from behind the bar. The only other person there at this late an hour was the new guy at the front. They ignored him and dashed to the back doors that led out into the courtyard.

CHAPTER 15

Fight Scene

Valentine and Trudi burst through the back doors of the Grande Chateau, running at full clip into the snow. A set of footprints pockmarked the deep drifts leading to and from the storage shed out near the edge of the woods. Travel was slow once they began trudging through the drifts, with each step sinking down to Valentine's upper thigh. The two shivered from the cold, but pressed onward.

Out of breath and sucking in cold air, they reached the shed. Faint light was emanating from a small window at the side of the building.

Valentine pulled on the door. "It's locked."

"Is someone there?" came a faint voice from inside. "If you're my assailant I have to warn you that even though I'm tied to a chair my fists are registered as deadly weapons!"

"J.J., it's us!" Valentine shouted. "Hang tight! We're gonna get you outta there!"

"Can't you pick the lock?" asked Trudi.

"That's a J.J. skill set. He could probably talk me through it from the other side of the door but the lockpick's in his satchel."

"J.J.!" Trudi yelled, "is there any way you can unlock the door from the inside?"

145

"No dice. I got a little overzealous with phone calls and ended up on the floor. I'm still tied to a chair, if that helps."

It didn't help. Valentine and Trudi circled the shed, looking for a usable point of entry. Upon spotting the tiny window, Valentine pointed at it.

"If I give you a boost, will you be able to make it through?"

"I can try," Trudi replied.

Trudi put her foot into Valentine's interlocked fingers, braced herself on his shoulders, and he lifted her up. She tried the latch on the window. "It's locked. Do we have anything to smash it with?"

Trudi hopped down and they searched for a rock in the snow by the woods. Finding one, Valentine hurled it at the window.

"Watch out!" he yelled as shattered glass showered on top of J.J.

"How many times do I have to tell you?" J.J. bellowed from his position on the floor, "Yell 'watch out' and *then* throw the dangerous thing!"

Valentine hoisted Trudi up once more. She picked the remaining pieces of glass out of the frame and was just small enough to slide through the small opening. She hooked her arm into a water pipe that ran across the ceiling and used it to swing down gracefully onto the floor of the shed. J.J. was tied to a chair resting on its side.

"Hey," he said.

Looking into the far back corner, Trudi gasped at the frozen body of Wallace P. Gross.

"Oh yeah," said J.J. "I figured he got stored here so he wouldn't be a bother to the hotel patrons. Grim stuff, right?"

Trudi went over to the door and unlocked it, letting Valentine in. He immediately grimaced at Wallace P. Gross's body. "Cold storage?" he asked.

"Yup," replied J.J.

The two lifted J.J. upright before beginning to untie him.

"How'd you get here?" Valentine asked.

"I don't know. I was knocked out and then I woke up here tied to this chair."

"Did you get a good look at whoever did it?" Trudi asked.

"Negative. They came at me from behind and caught me unawares. Look, can you two just get me out of here? We'll solve the Mystery of Who Knocked Me Out and then Tied Me Up in a Kill Room once we get to safety."

Trudi finished untying the ropes around his legs before moving up to help Valentine with the knot binding J.J.'s wrists.

"Hurry up, will you?" said J.J.

"I'm sorry, I cut my nails before we left and this is a really tight knot."

"Oh, come on. Trudi, will you give the guy a hand?"

"Calm down," said Trudi, "we'll get you out of here as soon as—"

The door creaked open. Standing there was the groundskeeper. He sneered at the children, his heaving breaths visible in the cold.

"Well, I guess we solved the Mystery of Who Knocked Me Out and then Tied Me Up in a Kill Room," said J.J.

The groundskeeper growled and reached for a shovel on the wall. Holding it in both of his hands, he pulled backward, ready to strike.

"Untie me untie me untie me!" J.J. screamed.

The groundskeeper swung with all of his might. Trudi and Valentine dove out of the way in either direction. The shovel connected with J.J.'s shoulder, knocking him back down onto the floor.

"Ow!" J.J. yelled while he tried to use his free legs to right himself. "You guys are gonna have to do this without me on account of that I'm tied to a chair! Scratch out his eyes like you're a wild chimpanzee!"

Valentine turned to his brother. "What?"

"You're a feral animal trapped in a corner! Unleash the beast!"

While Valentine was distracted, he didn't notice the groundskeeper raise the shovel above his head, ready to smash it down on the unsuspecting boy.

Trudi saw this happening and had time to react. She sized up the groundskeeper, searching for any exploitable weaknesses. If she had something sharp she could pierce that man's jugular vein and it would only take him about a minute to bleed out. Alternatively, she could slice his femoral artery with similar results. One well-placed palm thrust into his nose would drive cartilage into his brain cavity. That might be cool.

Instead, Trudi ran at the groundskeeper and jumped with all her might. She managed to hook both of her arms around his neck and hung on for dear life as he tried to shake her off. She resembled a cape on the back of a very homicidal and unfairly-sized superhero.

With the groundskeeper distracted by the Trudi de la Rosa Rodeo, Valentine launched himself at the gargantuan man and turned his body to deliver as much power to his right cross as possible, missing the man's face entirely and connecting with his shoulder.

The groundskeeper swung around and clubbed Valentine square in the chest with Trudi's flailing legs, sending him flying backward into his brother, who had only just now made it to his feet.

The collision sent J.J. crashing into the ground, shattering the wooden chair he was bound to into splintered ruins.

J.J. got up as quick as he could. Hands still tied to his back, but free from his prison, his eyes widened. "Now we're talking!" He lowered his head and charged at the groundskeeper like a raging bull, screaming, "Unleash the beast!"

He dove headfirst toward the man's stomach, connecting with his sternum with a resounding thud. The force of the blow knocked the shovel out of the groundskeeper's hand and propelled him backward into the wall, squishing Trudi and forcing her to lose her grip. She slid down to the floor in a daze.

The groundskeeper roared and grabbed J.J. by the neck, lifting him off his feet. J.J. struggled against him, but couldn't reach the man.

"J.J., hang on!" Valentine charged. He made it only as far as the groundskeeper's oversized hands before his own neck was caught in its grip. His manicured fingernails were not enough to free himself from the stranglehold.

The groundskeeper held the brothers in his grip and raised his arms above his head in a tremendous display of strength. Kicking and squirming as much as they could, the boys could only see the grimacing expression on the groundskeeper's face as they each fought to break his hold.

Face turning red and stars shooting in his eyes, J.J. attempted his last futile kicks in an effort to dislodge himself. *So this is how it ends*, he thought. *J.J. Watts and his best friend who just wanted to make an honest buck. They bit off more than they could chew and found their fate in a sorry mountain shed. A tragedy, and a very boring one at that.*

The lights in his eyes dimmed and a resigned comfort flooded his brain before he slipped into unconsciousness.

CLANG!

The sound came from behind the groundskeeper, reverberating around the tiny room with a sick echo. The groundskeeper's eyes crossed and his grip around the boys' necks loosened. He fell to his knees, releasing the two boys.

Gasping for breath on the floor of the shed, Valentine saw the groundskeeper waver on his knees before falling face-first and landing in front of him with a crash.

"Good swing," said Valentine between heavings of air. J.J. was unconscious on the floor, his arms tied behind his back. He was breathing.

Valentine gave him a few light slaps on the face. His eyes fluttered, he mumbled some words, and then stood bolt upright.

"I ain't done yet!" J.J. delivered a dazed headbutt into his brother's jaw.

"Jeez!" Valentine shouted. He gave his brother one last slap for good measure. This last one did the trick and the world came into focus for J.J.

He looked around the room.

"Did we win?"

"Yeah, we won," said Valentine.

"How'd I defeat him? My memory's a little fuzzy."

"He choked you until you passed out. Trudi saved us via shovel."

"Did I kill him?" Trudi asked fearfully.

Valentine examined the man on the floor and saw his body heaving up and down. "No, you just knocked him out."

Trudi screamed and raised the shovel over her head, ready to deliver the final blow. Valentine dashed over to her and put a hand on the shovel to prevent her from doing any more damage. "Easy, champ," he said. "Ghost Hunters Adventure Club doesn't kill."

"Yeah, well, I was thinking about revising that rule," J.J. said. He propped himself up on his knees and pulled himself upright with the help of the workbench. "C'mon, guys, we gotta tie this guy up, get moving, and find the next clue."

His knees buckled and he dropped to the floor.

Valentine rushed over to him. "You gotta rest for a bit. You're in no shape to be solving this mystery right now."

"Says you," said J.J. "My body's made of tougher stuff than this and there's a life-changing amount of treasure around the corner."

"J.J., come on. Don't make it about the treasure."

"We don't have time to argue," J.J. snapped. He found his footing and grabbed his satchel from the workbench, making sure it retained all of the items that he had put in there. "The next clue's under the bench Marcella always sat on. That's what the decoded message told us. It's Wallace P. Gross's manuscript, which will tell us everything we need to know to find the treasure."

"And his murderer," said Valentine.

"Trudi, we're gonna need that shovel." J.J. walked to the doorway, stopped, and turned to the others. "You guys coming or what?"

Valentine and Trudi followed J.J. out into the snow after tying the groundskeeper's hands behind his back and barring the door to the shed with the ice pick from the wall.

CHAPTER 16

The Chapter Where You Find Out Who Did It

J.J., Valentine, and Trudi trudged through the deep snow toward the statue of the angel near the chateau. None of them were dressed for the occasion. J.J.'s teeth were chattering but he pressed onward fearlessly. The stars were made visible by the breaking clouds up above and there remained an odd stillness to the cold outdoors.

Almost all of the lights were finally darkened in the chateau. Everyone must have turned in for the night.

J.J. reached the statue first. He searched his memory for the first time they had met Marcella P. Gross and triangulated the location of the now-buried bench.

"It should be right here. Trudi, lemme see that shovel."

Trudi handed him the shovel and shivered with her arms crossed while J.J. worked. He plunged the shovel into the hardened snow and pulled out a chunk, discarding it off to the side. As soon as he got tired, he handed the shovel to Valentine, who dutifully began digging.

Before hypothermia set in, Valentine struck dirt beneath the bench. He created a larger hole by scooping around the ice and plunged the shovel once again into the earth. It wasn't long before it struck something.

"That's gotta be it!" J.J. shouted. He and Trudi jumped into the hole and scooped out clumps of dirt with their hands. After a moment, J.J. was able to reach his hands around a handle. Grasping it, he pulled backward to reveal what they had been looking for.

J.J., Valentine, and Trudi stared at the leather, dirt-encrusted suitcase in J.J.'s hands.

"What are you waiting for?" asked Valentine.

J.J. tried to flip open the locks on the briefcase to no avail. Examining it from the side, he found a combination lock with a scrambled code on it.

"Not again!" he cried. "Why can't Wallace go easy on us for once?"

"We solved the last ones," said Trudi, "so we're smart enough to solve this one. What are we looking at here?"

The three of them studied the combination lock.

"Looks like we need a four letter combination," said J.J. "Choices are A-Z."

"Have you tried AAAA?" asked Trudi.

"Not unreasonable." J.J. scrolled all of the tumblers to "A" and tried the lock. "No dice. You want me to try AAAB?"

"There's gotta be another way," said Valentine.

"Wallace wouldn't just give us a code without a way to solve it," Trudi pointed out.

"Well, he did on the last one. It ended up being a Caesar salad or something. Marcella helped me solve it."

"Do you mean a Caesar cipher?" asked Valentine. "Because that's relatively easy to solve without a key."

Trudi thought for a moment. "With four wheels and twenty-six different letters per wheel, there'd be over 450,000 possibilities. We'd freeze to death before we even got to ten thousand. There's gotta be something in Wallace's past he had told you that could give you a hint as to what this might be."

"What about THAD?" Valentine suggested.

"Also not unreasonable." J.J. input "THAD" into the combination. The lock didn't budge.

"Well," he said, picking up the shovel, "for the sake of our numb toes and the limited time we've got to solve this mystery, I'm going to assume that Wallace P. Gross's solution to this puzzle was 'break the lock with a shovel.'"

Trudi shook her head. "But you could damage whatever's inside there."

"Oh come on, when was the last time you heard about a shovel irreparably damaging a manuscript?" J.J. raised the shovel over his head and aimed toward the briefcase.

"Wait!" Valentine hooted. "I've got it!"

* * *

THE ROOF OF THE GRANDE CHATEAU had remained entirely unoccupied for the duration of the story, up until now. The door to the roof creaked open and footfalls fell on gravel, scratching sounds coming from the floor. Creeping along slowly, the figure walked past the outcroppings of the chateau and worked their way toward the roof's edge.

* * *

"IT'S LCBS," SAID VALENTINE.

J.J. and Trudi looked at him quizzically.

"Less reasonable than the last two," said J.J., "but you've piqued my interest." He input "L, C, B, S" into the combination lock and the briefcase clicked open. J.J. looked at his brother.

* * *

RESTING THE RIFLE ON THE LIP OF THE ROOF, the figure steadied it against the wind and stared down the crosshairs. Between the sights were the children in the courtyard below.

* * *

"Library, Courtyard, Ballroom, Study," said Valentine. "It's the order Wallace showed us during the tour. Remember how he made a point of telling us the letter that each one started with and we both looked at each other like he was two sticks short of a hockey game?"

"That sly dog was really giving us a clue," J.J. said in admiration. "Wallace, you continue to impress me from beyond the grave."

They once again crowded around the briefcase while J.J. unhinged the locks and lifted the top case open. Inside was a stack of papers, bound together with brass tacks. The front page read,

THE SECRET OF THE GRANDE CHATEAU
BY WALLACE P. GROSS

"This is it!" Trudi exclaimed.

"What does it say?" asked J.J.

From the distance came a thundering crack, then a whistle, and the snow beside them shot into the air. A small crater had formed near J.J.'s head.

"Was...that a gunshot?" said J.J.

Another crack, another whistle. J.J. felt a searing pain in his left arm and looked down to see the red streak across his bicep. He had been grazed.

"That's a gunshot," he said. "Everybody scramble!"

They bolted out of the hole they had dug and ran in three different directions; J.J. toward the chateau, Valentine toward the shed, and Trudi toward the woods, clutching the manuscript of Wallace P. Gross tightly to her chest.

"Where's it coming from?" Valentine shouted.

Another thunderous crack, and a bullet whizzed down and punctured the snow in front of J.J.'s feet. He looked up to spot the muzzle of the gun pointing at him from the roof.

"It's coming from the chateau roof!" He dashed through the snow as fast as the deep drifts would allow him. "Find cover!"

Trudi dove behind a snow embankment by the edge of the forest. She saw both J.J. and Valentine were now running toward her. "Over here!"

"Run in a serpentine pattern!" J.J. screamed as another bullet whistled past his head. "Serpentine! Serpentine!"

Valentine made it to Trudi's safe embankment. He slid through the snow and hunkered down next to her, making sure to keep his head down below the drift. "Come on, J.J.!"

"I'm coming!" J.J. zigged and zagged as fast as he could through the snow. Another crack splintered through the cold air, shattering the head of the angel statue he had just passed.

Panicking, he dove headfirst behind the safety of the statue, its base barely visible above the snow. His heart pounded in his chest. He looked over to where Trudi and Valentine were hiding.

"Well, we're in cover," he said. "Now what?"

"Come to us!" shouted Valentine.

"I hear what you're saying, and I understand *why* you'd want me to come to you, but I've made the executive decision to stay here based on the bullets currently being shot at me."

"We've gotta get away from the chateau," said Trudi. "Why don't we make a break for the woods?"

"In this weather without proper clothing, we'd freeze to death in under an hour," replied J.J.

"He's right," Valentine said to Trudi. "We need to find another way out of here."

"Trudi," J.J. called, "got any ideas?"

Trudi searched her mind, then her eyes lit up. "J.J.! Remember how we saw that vent in the secret passageway before we fell through the wooden planks? There must be an entrance here in the courtyard!"

"That sounds awesome! I'll let you know when I can start searching around after this person stops shooting at me."

"Check the base of the statue!" Trudi shouted back.

J.J. seemed to get it. He dug at the base of the statue with his bare hands, sifting through layers of dirt and half-melted snow. He uncovered a grated vent where the statue met the ground. His hands were numb. "I've got something here! It's like what we found in the ballroom. And there's nothing blocking it."

"We'll come to you!" Valentine moved to get up but Trudi put her hand on his shoulder.

"The shooter might have a bead on us. J.J., is there any way you can distract them?"

J.J. took a deep breath. "Let the record state that I'm willing to put my life on the line for my friends!" He jumped out of his hiding place and waved at the assailant on the chateau roof. "You're a terrible shot, milk breath!"

He immediately dove back behind the angel statue, narrowly avoiding a bullet that would have pierced his heart a moment sooner.

"Now!" shouted J.J.

Trudi and Valentine got up from their embankment and raced toward the statue, sliding behind the base of the angel just before another shot rang out.

"Couldn't stand to be away from me, huh?" asked J.J.

"Not now," Valentine snapped. "Where's this exit?"

J.J. pointed to the metal vent by his feet. It was just wide enough for them to slide into one by one.

Valentine wrapped his fingers around the metal grate and pulled. "It won't budge and all these screws look tight. Is there a rock or something we can hit it with?"

"Back by where we were just hiding there might've been a few," Trudi said.

"If we can't get into here, it'll be suicide to make a break for the chateau."

"Wait," said J.J., "I know what we can use to open it." He reached into his satchel and produced the motorcycle kickstand. "I knew this would come in handy eventually."[3]

Valentine was shocked. "I thought we sold that for gas."

"I stole it back." J.J. jammed the kickstand between the metal grates and found a spot to use as leverage, pulling with as much might as his numb fingers would allow.

Another shot rang out and clipped one of the angel's wings. Rock and dust showered onto them.

"We need to hurry!" Trudi urged.

"Val, gimme a hand with this. I can feel it budging."

Valentine rushed to his brother's aid, grabbing an open portion of the kickstand and adding his strength to his brother's. Another crack of thunder and a showering of dust burned their eyes.

"Are they trying to bring the statue down on us?" coughed J.J. in a panic.

"I don't want to stick around long enough to find out," replied Trudi.

Valentine and J.J. gave another mighty pull. The screws that held in the vent began separating from the stone into which they were drilled. The more it gave way, the more leverage they could get. Shots kept ringing out, striking the angel statue in the leg. Before long the statue was

---

[3] Dr. Cecil H.H. Mills, author of this book, checking in again. I promise I'll be shorter this go-around. I received a note from my agent in an earlier draft of this book stating that this motorcycle kickstand revelation was a little too deus ex machina. For those unaware, this means the children were saved by a seemingly random and non-foreshadowed act of God, and by extension is a suggestion that I am a bad author.

I only disagree with people when they're wrong, so I'd like to take this paragraph to remind you that I guaranteed the motorcycle and its kickstand will not be mentioned again in this or any other book in chapter ten. This was what we intelligent authors refer to as a "classic misdirect." You thought it didn't have relevance to the story because I was speaking about it outside of the story. This was intentional. I lied to you. Here it is again. I am a good author.

Still, if you'd like to complain, I've included my P. O. Box info in the back matter of this book and will happily forward any hate mail you send over to my literary agent. I'm sure he'd love to hear from you.

standing like a religious flamingo liable to crush whatever was under it. With one final pull, the grate popped out and the brothers bent it further backward, creating a hole large enough to fit into.

"Trudi, you first!" J.J. urged.

She twisted her body to slide in, and with the help of the brothers dropped down safely into the secret passageway.

J.J. shoved Valentine down next. Another shot chipped away at the only remaining leg of the statue. Valentine slid through the grate and was caught on the other end by Trudi.

"Come on, J.J.!" Valentine called.

Another bullet cracked the leg of the statue and it began teetering. The structure now gone, the rest of the leg crumbled and tipped toward J.J. He dove headfirst down the grate, landing on Valentine and Trudi as the statue hit the ground and shattered. Large stone slabs now covered the grate, closing it off and enveloping the three in darkness.

It was a while before they moved. J.J. was the first to brush the broken bits of angel statue off of himself and stand up, coughing. Trudi looked down and saw the manuscript she was holding was still intact.

J.J. reached into his satchel and distributed three Grande Chateau-branded flashlights among the team. Valentine rested on his knees while Trudi flashed her beam down the hallway, illuminating the hole they had fallen into earlier in their adventure.

"J.J., you're bleeding," said Valentine, aiming his flashlight at the gash on his brother's arm.

With the adrenaline slowly leaving his bloodstream, J.J. could feel the throbbing heat emanating from his arm. He ripped off a strip of cloth from his undershirt and tied it in a knot around the wound. "All right," he said, "now there's nothing between us and the treasure. What does the manuscript say?"

"No," said Valentine, shaking his head, "I'm putting my foot down here."

J.J. cocked his head, looking at his brother. "What do you mean, no?"

"I'm done. When you told me we were going into the mystery business, you didn't tell me people were going to shoot at us. You didn't tell me that me and my friends might get killed. We were better off working drifter gigs in Harborville."

"Are you kidding? You were the one who wanted to keep going with this mystery in the first place."

"I wanted justice for Wallace P. Gross."

"You wanted to solve a mystery," J.J. retorted. "Don't you see how different the two are? I'm at least doing something practical by trying to find this treasure."

"What about the treasure?" said Valentine, growing more and more heated as he spoke. "You're the only one who cares about the money. You've only ever cared about money. I went along with this as long as I did because Wallace P. Gross's killer needed to be caught."

J.J. looked shocked. "I only care about the money? What I care about is putting food on the table. Truth isn't going to keep us from starving to death, and it sure as Christmas isn't gonna give us a place to sleep at night. Do you think I enjoy digging for clues in the freezing cold?"

"All you are is a con artist!" Valentine shouted at his brother. "We never should've come up here and we never should've tried to grift Wallace!"

"And all you are is a follower." J.J. didn't know how much he believed that, but he was angry now, and when he was angry he tended to hurt the people he cared about. "I don't need you," he went on. "You obviously don't care. If you're not committed to the mission then you're just dead weight."

Valentine's face felt hot. If he hated one thing, it was people accusing him of not caring. He collected himself, letting cold feelings make him say things he knew he would later regret.

"You and me, we're no detectives. We're just two idiots trying to get by. The best thing we could do right now is to go back up to the chateau, knock on Deputy Park's door, and hide there like the scared little kids we are until the real police come."

J.J. smirked. "I ain't stopping you, hotshot."

They stood there staring at each other until Valentine turned and walked away, rounding the hole in the floor and disappearing into the darkness of the hallway.

The rage that had filled J.J. dissipated. His arm hurt. He sank down to the floor amongst the rubble. "How the hell did we end up here?"

Trudi didn't know what to say.

"Congratulations, Trudi, you've been promoted," J.J. said glumly. "You're the new Valentine. You can take his name if you want; it'd save me a lot by not having to reprint business cards."

"I can't just take his name."

"Wasn't his to begin with. You think J.J.'s *my* real name?" J.J. got up and dusted himself off. "I guess it's just you and me and the treasure now. Let's go."

His legs felt heavy. The adrenaline had left his veins and his head buzzed. He leaned against the wall of the secret passageway. "Actually, let's take a quick break," he said, slumping down the wall and to the floor. "I'll only be a minute."

Trudi sat down next to him. She felt lost. Her life had spiraled out of control in the last few days. She figured all she had left was to sit here and wait with J.J., hoping they could make it out alive.

After a short while, J.J. felt the energy to stand up. He turned on his reserve charm that he pulled out when his main tank was empty. It was less convincing. "All right bud, it's time for the Ghost Hunters Adventure Club to ride once more on what could be their last and greatest mission. We go through the secret dungeon, we find the treasure, we get outta there. You ready?"

Trudi stood up too. "I guess I am."

"Not so fast," a voice said from across the hallway.

CHAPTER 17

A Reminder That Sometimes the Media Lies to You and I've Elected to Teach You This Life Lesson Because This Is the Actual Chapter Where You Find Out Who Did It

"Valentine, you're back!" J.J. stared at his brother from across the hole they had together created. "They always come crawling back. Well, I'm sorry to say, but Trudi is the new Valentine now. I don't know if we have a spot on our treasure hunting team for you anymore, but if you leave your resume with me I'll give you a call should we have any openings."

"We've got trouble." Valentine looked somber. His arms were raised slightly in surrender.

Out from behind him came Deputy Park.

"Deputy Park, how'd you find the secret passageway?" J.J. asked. "If you are arresting us for being down here I'd like to formally request trial by combat."

"What?"

Trudi looked the officer up and down. "I don't think he's here for that, J.J."

J.J. whirled to Trudi. "Prove me wrong."

"He has his hands up and he doesn't have his pistol in his holster."

J.J. turned back to Deputy Park and examined him. Sure enough, Trudi was right. The deputy was unarmed.

"You children are idiots," a familiar voice said from behind the officer. He stepped to the side, revealing Madame Fournier. A rifle was slung behind her back, which Trudi recognized as the one hanging in the lobby days earlier. In her right hand was Deputy Park's service revolver, now trained on them.

"Madame Fournier!" shouted J.J. "What are you doing down here?"

Valentine sighed. "She's the murderer."

"She's the...?" A blank expression formed on J.J.'s face as his brain disintegrated into a variety of oddly-shaped puzzle pieces. "...murderer?"

"Who, me?" Madame Fournier snickered. "I'm just a little old hotel manager. I don't know what you're talking about."

J.J. managed to reassemble the puzzle pieces in a socially acceptable amount of time. "You're the one who was watching Wallace. And you're the one who must have shot him when he was about to tell us everything."

"And the one who caught me down here and marched me back to you," added Valentine.

"I'd do it all again in a heartbeat if I had to," said Madame Fournier. "For years I've been searching for this treasure before Wallace caught wind of it and tried to take it. And now I have it all to myself."

"The Christmas you do," said J.J.

"You know, for as dumb as you all are, I'm impressed. You figured out how I killed Wallace, how I had the groundskeeper shatter the window to throw off the police. You just attributed it to the wrong suspects. I'll even give you points for finding and saving J.J. It's too bad it's come to this. Your attention to detail would make you all exceptional employees in the hotel hospitality business."

"Deputy Park," said Trudi, "what are you doing here?"

"I went up to the roof to investigate the gunshots."

"He thought they were fireworks," Madame Fournier explained.

"I thought they were fireworks. But the lady got the drop on me and led me down here. I'm sorry I didn't trust you about the secret passageway earlier."

"So now what?" asked J.J. "I assume you want the manuscript so you can go off and get the treasure for yourself?"

"Oh, I want the manuscript all right, but you're all coming with me. People have a knack for dying when they try to get through whatever John Henry Grande built down there, so I'm going to see if you four can solve it for me."

"Aw, man," said J.J. "I'd love to, but Valentine and I don't work together anymore. It's just me and New Valentine now." He shot a thumb over to Trudi for effect. "So we're just gonna climb up this grate back here and get out of your hair. Sorry, Old Valentine."

"Nice try, young man," said Madame Fournier.

"Aw man, you gave away my name?" Valentine said after J.J.'s words sunk in.

"Sorry," said J.J. Maintaining his defiance, he addressed Madame Fournier. "What if we don't come with you?"

"If you don't, then I march you all out into the snow and watch you freeze to death. It's a pretty good cover story, *n'est-ce pas*? Three miscreant teenagers find a rifle and use it to deface a priceless statue. Dutiful cop chases after them. They all get lost in the heavy snow and succumb to the elements just hours before the snow plows arrive."

J.J., Valentine, Trudi, and Deputy Park all grimaced. They knew that Madame Fournier had them in a corner.

"I guess we have to go along, then," said J.J. He looked over to his former brother, hoping he had a plan to get them out of this. Valentine was hoping the same from J.J.

"Who has the manuscript?" asked the hotel manager.

"I do." Trudi produced the pages tucked in her arm and fanned them out.

"Splendid," said Madame Fournier. "Shall we carry on?"

BEWARE
THE MONSTER
AT THE END
OF THE MAZE

CHAPTER 18

The Labyrinth

Madame Fournier led the Ghost Hunters Adventure Club and their uniformed compatriot down the slope created by the collapse of the first secret passageway. Making sure to keep them at a safe distance and within sight, she jumped down into the stone room.

J.J., Valentine, and Trudi looked around the room for the second time in as many days. J.J. spotted the words carved into the wall by the stone door.

BEWARE THE MONSTER AT THE END OF THE MAZE

"That isn't Wallace's handwriting," he whispered to Trudi.

"What?"

"I've seen his handwriting in his letter to Marcella. That's not his. Maybe it was written by John Henry Grande or another earlier explorer."

Madame Fournier tapped the tip of her pistol against the wall behind the team. "Secrets don't make friends, young adventurers."

Looking around the room, she spotted the long-ago-triggered spike trap, as well as the bones and tattered clothes of the victim it had claimed. "Clifton," she said. "So that's what happened to you."

171

"You knew this guy?" asked Valentine.

"He was the one who gave Wallace the idea in the first place. I...used to love him." She shook the thought from her head. "I would have killed him myself if he didn't happen to do so on his own." Madame Fournier shined her flashlight upon the stone door. "So how do we get past this?"

"Weren't you already past this door before?" asked Valentine. "Trudi heard digging and we barely escaped."

"That was the groundskeeper. He was strong enough to open the door by brute force. None of you are two hundred centimeters tall, so I assume we must take the smart route."

"Question," said J.J.

"Six foot seven," interjected Trudi.

Madame Fournier turned to Trudi, who was reading as fast as she could through Wallace's manuscript. "What does our dearly deceased author say, my darling?"

Trudi didn't bother to look up from her reading. "I don't know yet. So much of this is research into John Henry Grande and his life. What led him to gain his wealth and inevitably renounce it. If only I had more time to—"

"Trudi," Madame Fournier interrupted, tapping the wall behind her with the tip of her pistol again, "time is one thing we do not have."

Trudi fanned through the manuscript pages until she found a diagram of the room they were in. "To open the door, we have to input the right combination to affect the counterweight attached to it. J.J., go to that panel of holes on the left wall by the door."

J.J. followed Trudi's orders and shined his flashlight on the leftmost wall. He approached it, rubbing his palm across it to wipe away the dust and thick cobwebs. When this was complete, the wall showed several rows of holes, each about the size of a finger.

"There should be four rows and ten columns on the panel," said Trudi.

J.J. confirmed her notes. "So what do we do with this?"

"I'm gonna need you to stick your fingers in the holes of the corresponding numbers for the year of John Henry Grande's birth: 1876."

J.J. raised his hand to the holes, then stopped and asked Trudi, "What happens if I get the wrong hole?"

Trudi turned the page and gulped. "It says here that there's a mechanism behind the wall that, um…chops your finger off."

J.J. turned back to the panel, raised his finger up, then spun around to address the group. "You know, I'm gonna use my one veto to excuse myself from this puzzle and instead nominate Madame Fournier for the hole puncher job."

Madame Fournier snorted. "Keep dreaming, young man."

"The once-daily veto is a sacred institution!" J.J. protested. "But fine, have it your way. In that case I nominate Deputy Park for the hole puncher gig."

"Hey!"

"Come on, rookie, how many fingers do you really need to arrest people?"

"J.J.," said Madame Fournier, growing impatient, "put in the code."

J.J. took a deep breath and readdressed the panel. "Okay, okay, so these four columns represent the year and the ten rows represent the ten possible digits?"

"Starting from zero at the top and then counting up to nine," replied Trudi.

"All right," J.J. said. "1876, that should be easy." He counted down the column in the first position and raised his finger, perspiration forming on his forehead. Slowly, his finger traveled toward the hole, inching closer as J.J. worked up the nerve to commit.

"Are you sure 1876 isn't some sort of cryptic clue we have to decipher?" J.J. asked. "Wallace is known for that sort of stuff, you know."

"Oh my stars!" Madame Fournier growled. "Put your finger in the hole or I'll shoot it off for you."

"Fine, fine, I'll do it." J.J. took a deep breath and raised his finger toward the hole corresponding to "1." Closing his eyes and bracing for pain, he pushed his finger into the hole.

His fingertip felt a button and he heard an audible click. Pulling his finger out, he was happy to see it remained in one piece. "All right, that's one." He moved his finger to the "8" position on the second column. Holding his breath, closing his eyes, and bracing for pain, he inserted his finger.

Another click.

J.J. let out another sigh of relief. "Halfway there."

He raised his finger, positioned it at the "7" hole, held his breath, shut his eyes, braced for pain, and inserted his finger.

Another click, another sigh of relief.

"All right everybody, last one," said J.J., mostly to himself. He thought of all the good times he and his ten digits had had over the years, the things he was able to steal, the obscene gestures he could make...all of that. He would truly miss them if he were to lose one in a freak mystery-solving accident. Having properly reminisced about his fingers, he went for it, placing his index finger into the hole corresponding to "6."

J.J. let out an ear-shattering howl, yanked his finger back, and hunched over in pain. Valentine rushed to his former brother's aid. Madame Fournier and Deputy Park stood in place in shocked silence. Trudi read and reread the manuscript to find what she had gotten wrong.

"J.J., what happened?" asked Valentine.

J.J.'s shrieks of pain turned into laughter. He held up his hand: all five fingers still in place. "Come on guys, I'm just trying to lighten the mood," he said to the rest of the group. "It's bad enough we're stuck down here with a homicidal hotel manager. Try and live a little."

Deputy Park groaned.

Valentine punched J.J. on the shoulder. It wasn't a playful punch. "Not cool."

Something began creaking in the room. They turned to see the stone door slowly raising upward.

"Let's go," said Madame Fournier, ushering them into the next room.

Valentine punched J.J. on the shoulder once more before walking to the next room under the watchful eye of Madame Fournier, her pistol, and the intimidating rifle slung across her back.

The group filed into the next room. Madame Fournier stood in the doorway and had her four captive party members stand in front of her to prevent their escape.

"All right, Trudi," said the hotelier. "What's next?"

Trudi flipped through more pages of the manuscript as she walked toward the center of the room. "This is a pressure plate puzzle. It was too dark and I didn't know what I was looking for the last time I was in here, but there should be four different plates..." she referred to Wallace's writing again, "...in each corner of the room."

She walked to the end of the huge room toward the edge of where their flashlights could reach. Shining her light on the ground in the corner of the room, she spotted a square, carved stone panel inset within the floor. Leaning over to brush it off, she revealed an image.

"A mountain," she said. Shining her flashlight to the right of it, she revealed a hole about three feet deep next to the pressure panel. "This must've been where the groundskeeper was digging. He had the right idea. I think he was trying to dig beside the panel to find the mechanism beneath it in hopes of bypassing the puzzle altogether."

"That's pretty smart," said J.J. "He always struck me more as the ham-fisted, hit-you-with-a-shovel type. Maybe I read him wrong."

Trudi walked to another corner of the room where she uncovered another panel. "This one's supposed to represent a gold coin, meaning this one..." she said, walking to the next corner of the room and brushing off the dusty pressure plate on the floor, "...should be a skull."

Walking down to the last corner, she revealed the final pressure plate: a stone with the image of the chateau carved into it. "Okay. Now we just need to hit them in the order in which John Henry Grande lived these moments in his life. J.J., go to the mountain. Valentine, go to the chateau. Deputy Park, go to the skull. I'll take the gold coin."

Each person did as they were told and walked to their corresponding pressure plate. Madame Fournier remained standing by the door, barring anyone from escape.

"Everyone get on your hands and knees in front of your pressure plate," Trudi instructed. "Don't press it yet. On three, J.J. you're gonna hit the mountain, then Valentine you're gonna hit the chateau. Then Deputy Park you're gonna hit the skull that represents his death, then I'm gonna hit the gold coin which the manuscript says represents the treasure he left us. That all make sense, everybody?"

"Makes sense," said Valentine, although it didn't 100 percent make sense to him. If this was a pressure plate puzzle, it could conceivably be solved by one person walking from one plate to the next. So why was she having everyone get down on their hands and knees to press theirs?

Still, he trusted Trudi wouldn't lead them astray, so he kept his mouth shut.

Trudi got on her hands and knees in front of her pressure plate. "All right everybody, on three. One…two…"

"Wait!" Madame Fournier screeched. "Everyone meet by the door!"

Trudi cursed under her breath. She got up reluctantly and walked to meet the rest of the group where the hotelier had ordered them to.

"Very clever, Trudi. You almost got me." The hotelier had her pistol pointed directly at the former front desk receptionist. "Until I started wondering why you needed everyone on their hands and knees. Then I realized…" She pointed her flashlight at the walls of the cavernous room. All along them were small holes dotting the walls at chest height. "You were going to enter the combination wrong, which would have fired what I assume are arrows into me."

"Poison-tipped arrows," Trudi expounded.

"*Mon amie*, everyone knows John Henry Grande amassed his fortune as a mountaineer before he built the chateau, so naturally the solution to the puzzle would be mountain, coin, chateau, skull."

Trudi looked away, dejected.

"Follow me." Madame Fournier beckoned them with her gun as she walked to the first pressure point. "No crouching down, please."

She stepped on the first plate and it depressed into the ground with a clicking noise. She dragged the group along to the gold coin-inscribed plate and stepped on it without much fanfare. J.J. reflexively winced to brace for any arrows that might fly into him. Luckily, Fournier's choice seemed to be the correct one.

She went to the plate inscribed with the chateau, stepped on it, and it clicked without incident. "And now, finally, onto the last one." She stepped on the pressure plate with the skull inscribed on it. As soon as she depressed it all the way down, all four pressure plates began clicking, raising up to their original positions. As they rose, the team heard a rumbling at the end of the room.

A door appeared. First as cracks in the wall and then as the stone gave way and swung upward, a gaping hole that revealed steps leading downward.

"To the next room?" suggested Madame Fournier. Everyone turned to make their way down the steps. "One moment, Trudi."

Trudi turned to face Madame Fournier, who held the pistol under her chin. "No more tricks, darling. Do you understand?"

Trudi clenched her teeth. She hated being beat.

"I understand."

"Marvelous," said Madame Fournier. "Now let's go catch up with the group. We don't want to get lost, do we?"

Trudi and the hotel manager rejoined J.J., Valentine, and Deputy Park as they traversed down a spiraling staircase, which let out into a naturally-formed open chasm. The stone walls jutting out stood in stark contrast to the carved out room they had just exited.

"What's that sound?" asked J.J.

"I guess it's an underground river. Melting snow must run off into it," said Trudi.

"Wow. It's remarkable that this place has held up to the elements for all these years."

Then the ground gave way.

J.J., Valentine, Deputy Park, and Trudi tumbled downward in a shower of dust and rubble. Bouncing off the side of the chasm, J.J. grabbed onto a tree root protruding out of cracks in the rock. He saw Valentine had managed to do the same just above him.

Trudi and Deputy Park were lucky. She managed to grab onto the edge of the floor as it crumbled under her, leaving her only a short pull back to safety. She gave Deputy Park a hand up, both of them rolling over the edge and to safety.

"See, this is why I brought you all along," said Madame Fournier from the remains of the platform. She had stayed upright and un-tumbled by remaining at the back of the group. "Better you all than me, am I correct?"

"Please stop talking!" J.J. shouted from down the chasm. "We don't like you!"

Trudi leaned back over the edge, seeing him and Valentine hanging on for dear life.

"Guys, you okay?"

Valentine gripped whatever roots and soil he could, his dirt-encrusted fingers embedded deep within the soft soil surrounding the rock. He summoned the courage to look up at Trudi.

"Never better," he said.

The sound of rushing water was much louder now. J.J. looked down to see white peaks rushing past him, just barely visible in the darkness. "Old Val, we got a problem," he said. "Death drop below."

Valentine summoned more courage to look below him into a craggy and sharp and wet void of darkness. He gulped.

"It would appear as if the soil has eroded over years thanks to the river," said Madame Fournier. "I'd hurry out of there, if I were you. There's no telling where an underground river would spit you out, but it's a guarantee that wherever you ended up you'd be dead."

J.J. looked up to Valentine. "You gotta climb, dude!"

Valentine's handhold on the bundle of roots he had been clinging to was slipping. He gripped tighter and tried to feel around with his legs for a foothold. "I'm kind of stuck here, but good suggestion."

J.J. sighed. "Fine, then I'm coming up." He grabbed hold of Valentine's leg and pulled himself upward. "Just hang in there, kitten."

Valentine didn't know how to process this. "What are you doing!"

"Just hang in there. If you let go we both die."

Valentine didn't have many choices here. He readjusted his grip, feeling tree roots snap as the weight of J.J. climbing up to his torso added to the load.

J.J. made it up above Valentine with great discomfort only to Valentine. He found a rock outcropping he could use as a hold and placed his foot onto his former younger brother's shoulder.

Valentine's muscles were cramping. The shoe digging into his shoulder did not help. He knew he didn't have long.

Looking to his left, J.J. saw under the floor of the hallway just in time to spot a rusted circular saw break away from the ground and fall into the river below with a faint splash. A menacing, swinging ax with a rotten wooden handle followed shortly after it.

"Trudi! What are sharp killing objects doing down here?"

Flipping through the pages of the manuscript, Trudi spotted the page of the current puzzle. "It was supposed to be a challenge of skill and agility," she called down. "We were supposed to be running through a gauntlet."

J.J. strained to keep himself attached to the chasm wall. "What's the connection to John Henry Grande's life here? Was his heart broken once by woodshop teacher?"

"Just climb back up!" Deputy Park leaned over the edge and extended a hand downward.

J.J. was close to the top, just out of reach of the deputy.

"Hold tight, Old Valentine!"

"What?" Valentine asked, right before J.J. placed his shoe over his face.

"I don't like this," said Valentine in what could be considered an understatement.

"Just need a little more leverage." J.J. used the extra few inches to jump up and grab Deputy Park's wrist.

The force of the push severed the remaining tree roots that held Valentine in place. He felt himself slipping as he tried to dive his hands back into the soil.

"J.J., I'm falling!

"Grab my leg, you dingus!"

Valentine launched himself upward with his last burst of strength, catching hold of J.J.'s ankle around his pants cuff.

Trudi jumped in to aid the deputy, grabbing J.J.'s other wrist. They worked in tandem and pulled with all their might.

First, J.J. appeared. He hooked his arm onto the safety of the platform and within moments rested his torso against the edge. He was close enough to the top where Valentine scrambled up next to him and grabbed hold of the floor. One final heave brought them to safety.

Both of them rolled onto their backs, gasping to catch their breaths.

J.J. looked over at Deputy Park, the man who had helped save his life. "Mention this to no one." He then glanced over at Valentine. "Thanks for letting me use your face."

Valentine got up, still huffing, and jabbed a finger at J.J. "Stop kidding around. I didn't even want to be down here and now this is probably my last day on Earth. If we ever make it out alive, I'll be happy to never see you again for the rest of my life."

J.J. was taken aback. "Jeez, Old Val, lighten up."

Valentine whirled around and stomped toward the next room over the edges of the missing hallway to avoid falling in again. The other four followed behind him, Madame Fournier bringing up the rear.

Traversing the hallway into the next room, Trudi read at a furious pace. The group stepped into a tight square room with a ceiling mere inches above their heads. Trudi looked up and her eyes widened.

"Valentine, watch out!"

Valentine turned his head to address Trudi, but felt his leg snag on something. Looking down, he saw a silver string just after it had been broken by his step.

"A tripwire!"

The walls around the team began trembling. A heavy stone door fell into place, trapping them in the room.

Then, silence.

"What's happening?" asked Deputy Park.

Trudi turned the page of her manuscript. She sighed deeply. "Bad stuff."

They heard a crackling sound coming from the ceiling and grains of sand began spilling out of the cracks above them. Slowly at first, but within moments a deluge of sand began pouring on the floor of the room. Before long, sand had risen up to their ankles. They were trapped.

"This room is filling with sand," Trudi announced needlessly. "We don't have long."

"What kind of puzzle is this?" J.J. shrieked.

"This isn't a puzzle," Valentine said grimly. "This is punishment." He immediately began examining every piece of wall in the small room. Every crack, every stone block. "Try to find a way out!"

Trudi ferociously examined the pages of the manuscript. Both she and Madame Fournier were up to their knees in sand.

"How do we escape this, Trudi?"

"I don't know! Wallace's manuscript had everything to solve the puzzles, but it doesn't say what to do if you fell for the trap."

Fournier aimed the pistol at Trudi and cocked back the hammer. "You're a smart girl. Figure it out."

Trudi gulped. The sand was at her waist now. J.J. and Valentine were clawing at the walls, trying to find a fingerhold that might save them. Deputy Park stood on top of the sand and tried his best to plug one of the holes from which the sand was flowing. He was fighting a losing battle.

"There's gotta be something!" Trudi shouted. "John Henry Grande had to have built a safety in case he accidentally triggered it himself."

"We don't have much to work off of here!" The sand was up to Valentine's chest now. "All I see is sand and walls and ceiling."

"The floor!" Trudi exclaimed. "There's gotta be a release in the floor somewhere!"

"How would we even check the floor?" J.J. yelled. "I'm not sure if you're aware, but there's sand on it!"

"Dig!"

With the sand up to his shoulders, Valentine dove down and displaced as much of the coarse material as he could with his hands. Holding his breath, he submerged himself in the sand, feeling around the floor with his eyes closed, running his fingers across stone bricks, feeling through the seams. When he couldn't hold his breath any longer, he fought back up to the surface. "Nothing here! Keep trying!" He waded through the neck-deep sand to a separate portion of the room to repeat the search. Fruitless again, he came up for air.

"I got nothing!" J.J. gasped after his own search.

"Me neither," replied Valentine.

Only inches separated those trapped in the room from the ceiling. J.J. dove down again, clawing his way through dense, heavy sand to reach the bottom. Deputy Park's head had just disappeared beneath one of the growing peaks.

Valentine struggled to stay above the sand, keeping his mouth breathing as he was about to kiss the ceiling. Trudi and Madame Fournier were both in the same position as he.

J.J. emerged from the sand.

"Valentine, I'm sorry. I'm so sorry I brought you here. You don't deserve this."

Valentine couldn't hear the rest of what J.J. said. He closed his eyes and took a deep breath as the sand enveloped him.

Blackness.

His heart pounded in his chest, his lungs aching for oxygen.

Then he heard a new sound, as if someone had pulled the stopper on a bathtub, and the sand shifted beneath them. He rose up and gasped for a breath. Trudi, Madame Fournier, and J.J. were doing the same.

The room was draining faster than it could be filled. Within moments the sand was back down to their necks.

"What happened?" asked Madame Fournier.

"I don't know," J.J. replied, stumped. "I didn't find anything down there."

When the sand reached their chests Deputy Park burst forth from underground. His chest heaved as he drew in air. "I found it! I found a loose stone and pulled as hard as I could!"

J.J. laughed in disbelief. "I can't believe you did it, Park!"

"Neither can I," replied the deputy, then he hacked some sand out of his lungs.

The team breathed a collective sigh of relief while the room drained of sand. Before long they were sitting against the walls on top of a thin layer of sand, waiting for their hearts to stop beating out of their chests.

Valentine looked at J.J., who looked back at him. There's a funny thing that brothers have where they don't need to say words for the other to understand what they're saying. What would have gone here would have been a long conversation where J.J. apologized for how he treated Valentine, admitting that his greed for the treasure had blinded him to the point where he risked the lives of the only people he gave a damn about in this world.

Valentine would then admit that he truly cared for J.J. and felt equally blinded by wanting to solve the secret of the Grande Chateau. They would acknowledge that they had to work together to get out of this situation alive, then would cap it off with their secret handshake.

Instead, they just nodded at each other.

Then a sound came from beyond the walls. A switch flipped. On the opposite end of the room, an exit revealed itself as a stone door lifted.

"There's the way to the next room," said Valentine.

Madame Fournier frowned. "What's next, Trudi? I don't want any more surprises like the one we just experienced."

"Nothing," Trudi answered.

"Nothing?"

Trudi flipped to the last page and closed the cover. "That was it. That was the last one. The treasure's in the next room."

"Give me that," the hotelier said. She snatched the manuscript from Trudi and flipped to the end, pistol still in hand. After a moment, she looked up.

"That *is* it. Well, let's get ourselves John Henry Grande's fortune."

CHAPTER 19

John Henry Grande's Fortune

Valentine and J.J. walked ahead of everyone else in hopes of being out of earshot of Madame Fournier. As the long hallway carved out of the natural rock turned a corner, they found their chance.

"Once she gets the treasure she won't have any use for us," said J.J.

"I know," Valentine said. "If we have any hope for getting out of this we gotta get working on some plans quick."

"If it comes to it, I'm gonna rush Madame Fournier. I probably won't make it, but it'll give you the space you need to overpower her and save Trudi and Deputy Park."

"That's weird."

"What?"

"That's the first time I've heard you put someone else's needs ahead of your own."

J.J. shook his head. "Yeah, well, don't let anyone think I'm going soft, all right?"

"I'm hoping you won't have to rush anyone. There's still something that's bothering me, but it might be our way out."

"What's that?"

"The monster at the end of the maze."

* * *

THE NARROW HALLWAY SOON OPENED UP, spilling out into a large, domed room. J.J. shined his flashlight toward the ceiling, revealing the colossal rock formation they had entered. Stalactites hung from its roof, dripping condensation down to the floor. This cave was the largest room that they had been in since they started their descent into the mountain.

"What the hell could've made this?" asked Deputy Park.

"It was probably naturally formed long before John Henry Grande found it," Trudi said. "Grande probably discovered it while he was exploring the mountain and turned the pathway that led to it into his maze."

"So this is the last room," said Madame Fournier, examining the stone walls. "Where's your treasure, Grande?"

Madame Fournier shone her flashlight across the room. It rested upon a large wooden chest at the top of a platform. A small staircase was carved into the rock leading up to it. "There you are…"

A thought flashed in Valentine's mind. He had an idea.

"J.J., go get the treasure."

"Don't needa tell me twice." J.J. moved toward the chest at the other end of the room, but was stopped in his tracks by Madame Fournier's voice.

"Wait one second," she said.

"Fine," said Valentine. "Then I'll go myself." He began walking with confidence toward the raised platform. Madame Fournier hurried with her pistol drawn to position herself between the group and the treasure.

Pointing the gun at Valentine, she barked, "Fall back in line, soldier."

Valentine raised his arms and clenched his teeth, maintaining eye contact with the hotelier while he backed up to the rest of the group.

"You know something I don't know, don't you?" said Madame Fournier. "What makes you want to get to that treasure so badly?"

"What makes *you* want to get to that treasure so badly?" parroted J.J. in an annoying French accent.

Valentine shot a glance at his brother. "Don't do this now, J.J."

"Why? Do you think I'm gonna give away the secret?"

To Madame Fournier, who did not possess the same sort of brother telepathy previously mentioned, this exchange fell in line with what she had previously experienced with the brothers—useless bickering.

"Trudi," she snapped, "what's going on?"

Whether she simply deduced it from the brothers' language or some of that brotherly telepathic energy had rubbed off on her over the past couple days, Trudi turned impassive as well. "I don't know what you're talking about, Madame Fournier."

"Back up! All of you!" said Madame Fournier, waving her pistol from person to person. "If anyone gets close to me, that's the end for them. Do you understand?"

Deputy Park gulped. He saw no way out of this. He had spent the last several days away from home at the Grande Chateau and missed his wife dearly. He shivered at the thought of never seeing her face again.

Madame Fournier inched backward until her foot found the first step up to the platform. She didn't dare take her eyes off of her four captives at this moment. Step by step up the cold stone, she worked her way ever closer to the treasure of John Henry Grande.

Reaching the top of the step, she searched again with her foot for the base of the chest. She found the lock with her free hand. It was open.

"All right, let's see what sort of treasure John Henry Grande has in store for us."

She broke eye contact for a brief moment to unhinge the latch of the chest and peer at the contents inside. Her eyes darted back to Valentine.

"It's empty."

A thin smile formed across Valentine's lips.

"What kind of game are you playing?" Madame Fournier looked back down to the chest and threw the top open, revealing its empty contents. She couldn't hear it herself, but within the treasure chest a tumbler clicked into place.

Valentine stared directly at the hotel manager. The one who had killed Wallace P. Gross, had tried to kill him and his friends, and who had forced them all through this maze at the risk of their own lives. Given the chance, he knew she would kill them all and feel no remorse over it.

"Beware the monster at the end of the maze," he said.

Madame Fournier furrowed her brow in confusion. "What?"

A loud, muffled boom sounded just beyond the walls. Followed by another boom, followed by yet another boom, and the ground trembled beneath them.

All at once, cracks formed throughout the cave, evolving into an increasingly dangerous fissure that bifurcated the room between Madame Fournier and her captives.

J.J., Valentine, Trudi, and Deputy Park felt the ground crumbling beneath them.

"Back up, everybody!" J.J. screamed before the floor he was standing on all but disintegrated. Valentine, Trudi, and Deputy Park jumped back in step. Crumbling rocks began dislodging themselves from the ceiling of the cave.

"The whole room's coming down! Get back to the hallway!" Valentine bellowed mid-dash.

Madame Fournier immediately jumped into action, dashing as fast as she could toward safety. With each step the foothold she found would almost instantaneously disappear. She dropped the pistol in a leap toward steady ground and watched it plummet into the dark chasm below.

Out by the entrance to the cavern, the four dove for safety. The narrow hallway appeared as if it would hold.

Madame Fournier leapt from falling rock to falling rock, dodging stalactites haphazardly falling around her.

There was a version of J.J. who would have enjoyed this. One who would have taken delight in the suffering of the person who had tried to kill him and his friends.

But *this* J.J. was no longer *that* J.J. *This* J.J. wanted Madame Fournier to receive the justice she deserved.

"You're not getting away that easily!" he shouted as he sprang into the cavern.

"J.J., wait!" Valentine stared in shock. "It's too dangerous!"

J.J. either didn't hear him or pretended not to. He ran at a full sprint toward Madame Fournier, uncaring of what heavy thing could be falling on top of him at any moment.

Madame Fournier was fighting a losing battle. She leapt from rock to rock, but couldn't gain ground against the cave's crumbling. The soft, cloudy light of daybreak washed in through the half-lost ceiling. She made one last desperate dive toward the stable ground before her.

Her fingertips fell just inches short.

J.J. saw this and dove headfirst toward the newly created cavern. He slid on the ground, hooking one of his arms into whatever crumbled rock would brace him. With the other hand he reached as far as his arms would allow, grasping at whatever he could save.

He felt a snag. The room finally settled as the last pieces of the cave sloughed off into the ground hundreds of feet below.

Valentine saw his brother dangling from the ledge, unmoving. He dashed over to him.

"J.J.! What's wrong?"

"Just help me with this, will ya?"

Valentine grabbed J.J.'s shoulders and pulled backward with all his might. It was then he saw what they were pulling. Up from the chasm, with his hand firmly gripped around the shoulder strap of the ornate rifle that was once meant to murder them, J.J. held onto Madame Fournier.

With another strong pull, they dragged her up to safety. She lay on the floor, coughing from the dust and exertion.

J.J. and Valentine fell to the ground themselves, out of breath and exhausted. Trudi and Deputy Park ran over.

"You...s-saved my l-life..." Madame Fournier stammered as she got up off of her knees.

J.J. and Valentine were in the process of getting up themselves. "Don't..." J.J. huffed, "...don't mention it."

"I'll make sure you regret it!" Madame Fournier whipped the butt of the rifle into J.J.'s stomach. He doubled over in pain. In one quick moment she had the rifle against her shoulder and ready for action.

"Now which of you dies first?"

She didn't even have time to hear a response. Seeing the move against J.J., Deputy Park rushed to Madame Fournier's side and, with the strength and precision of a well-trained officer of the law, he karate chopped her in the throat.

Madame Fournier dropped her rifle and fell to her knees, reaching for her throat as she wheezed in air.

"I was really itching to use that move," said Deputy Park.

J.J., still doubled over in pain, gave a weak thumbs up to the deputy. "I owe you one, Officer." He rolled onto his back, wincing. "And I want you to know how rarely I owe officers of the law one. This is a real honor for you."

For the first time in days, sunlight peeked above the horizon and through the clouds in the open air of the chasm beneath them. The cave they were once in had existed at the very edge of a cliff on Grande Mountain. Whatever explosives John Henry Grande had placed years ago had shorn off the roof of the place.

In the distance, visible just above the rocks behind them, was the Grande Chateau.

CHAPTER 20

Snowplow Cometh

Driving up the road of Grande Mountain, now bathed in sunlight that was doing its slow work to melt the ice, was the ever-faithful snowplow. With its plow to the ground and salt granules being ejected from its hindquarters, it paved a welcome path all the way up to the Grande Chateau. Finally being released from their admittedly comfortable and amenable prison, patrons of the chateau cheered at the sight of the machine.

Following closely behind the snowplow was a news van, the letters "WHAB" emblazoned on the side in red.

It took the news crew mere minutes to set up lights just outside the entrance of the chateau, moving like clockwork as they fired up their Fresnel lenses and placed diffusion flags on c-stands to soften it.

When that was finished, a woman in a purple blazer stepped in front of the camera. She gave herself a countdown before she spoke.

"Murder and mystery on Grande Mountain," she started. "I'm here on-site at the Grande Chateau where a freak snowstorm trapped the residents of the resort over the long weekend. But more interesting than being held hostage by the weather? The weekend began with a murder.

"Noted mystery author Wallace P. Gross died under mysterious circumstances just as the snowstorm hit, and we're told that the real killer wouldn't have been found were it not for the efforts of three young adventurers."

The camera pulled back and revealed J.J., Valentine, and Trudi. They hadn't had time to clean themselves up and remained as dirty and disheveled as they were down in the caves. J.J. checked the bandage on his arm to make sure it hadn't started bleeding again.

"Tell me in your own words," said the reporter, "what happened this weekend at the Grande Chateau?"

J.J. stepped forward and leaned into the microphone. "Thank you for taking the time to speak with us, Carly. I've been a longtime fan of your venerable news channel and the nuanced, intelligent reporting contained within."

"Just answer the question, please."

"Right, well, myself—that's J.J. Watts-W-A-T-T-S—and the rest of the Ghost Hunters Adventure Club, Harborville's foremost authority on private investigation and paranormal phenomena—that'd be my brother Valentine Watts and our new cohort Trudi de la Rosa—"

"All we need is a sound bite, kid."

"All right, all right. We were initially called up here by Wallace P. Gross himself, and while through no circumstance of our own did he meet his grisly fate, we worked together to unravel the mystery and identify the real culprit. With the help of…" he sighed, "Harborville's finest, we were able to track down this culprit through a maze of subterranean passageways and eventually apprehend her."

"Now, just who was the killer here, and why did she want Wallace P. Gross dead?"

"Ma'am, the 'why' is a complicated answer. But if you want to ask the culprit herself, she's right over there."

J.J. pointed to a waiting police car with its door open. Being led out by Deputy Park in handcuffs were Madame Fournier and the groundskeeper.

"Hey, Fournier!" J.J. taunted. "How do the cuffs fit?"

Madame Fournier scowled at J.J. "You haven't seen the last of me, Ghost Hunters Adventure Club! I'll get you if it's the last thing I do!"

"Yeah, well, bite me," said J.J.

The camera swung back to J.J. "I don't even think she's actually French. Anyway, as I was saying, we're the Ghost Hunters Adventure Club and we'll take on any job, big or small. From haunted bar mitzvahs to haunted global conspiracies, we've got you covered. That's G-H-O-S-T—"

The reporter stepped into frame and addressed the camera. "Thank you for speaking with us today. I'm Carly Contreras with WHAB."

The cameraman lowered his camera. Carly lit a cigarette and turned to J.J. "Mindfulness meditation will do wonders for you, kid."

With that, the news crew packed up, leaving J.J., Trudi, and Valentine alone. They walked back into the lobby of the chateau.

"That could've gone worse," said Valentine. "You didn't swear this time."

"Yeah, I hope we can at least get some exposure out of it. Ghost Hunters Adventure Club, Incorporated, operated at a net loss this weekend."

"There'll be other mysteries to solve," said Trudi. "You two seem to have a knack for getting yourselves into trouble."

"I'll take that for the compliment that I choose to see it as," said J.J. "Are you sure you don't want to join up with us? I can't guarantee it'll be lucrative but I *can* guarantee a life less ordinary."

"I'm sure," she said. "With Fournier gone, this chateau is in complete disarray. They'll need someone to whip it back into shape."

"The Ghost Hunters Adventure Club!" came a familiar voice. They looked up to see Thad Newbury and Marcella P. Gross descending the grand staircase at the other end of the room.

"Ah, the two lovebirds," said J.J. "About all the trouble we gave you back there—"

"It's water under the bridge, I suppose," said Marcella. "I think we all got the closure that we needed out of this weekend, whether we wanted to get it or not."

"So what really happened down there?" asked Thad.

"Well," started Valentine, "Wallace was smart enough to point us in the direction of the treasure and had faith in us to figure out that the treasure didn't exist. John Henry Grande was driven mad by his wealth and saw it as the source of all his unhappiness. I guess he built the cave to punish anyone who might have chased greed the way that he did."

"Yup," said J.J., turning red. "I definitely knew that."

"The fact of the matter," said Valentine, "is that Wallace P. Gross gave us all the clues we needed to solve this, even though he knew he was going to die. He was a remarkable man."

"He will be missed," said Marcella. Some human emotion tried to appear on her face, but she managed to suppress it. "Well, we're on our way out. You kids take care, okay?"

"We will, ma'am," replied Trudi.

Thad raised his eyebrows above his sunglasses. "Say, would you kids maybe be interested in novelizing the events of this weekend? It could make some big waves in the Young Adult world."

"Thanks, Mr. Newbury," said J.J., "but our good friend Dr. Cecil H.H. Mills takes care of that stuff for us, that handsome rogue."

"I see," said Thad. "Well, don't hesitate to call if you need anything. And Valentine, please let me know once you've finished the first draft of *Boob Quest*. I'm *very* eager to give that a read."

"You got it, Mr. Newbury."

Thad and Marcella walked out toward the lobby exit, hand in hand.

J.J. watched them go. "I one day aspire to be either that venomous or that stupid. Those two have very admirable qualities about them."

"J.J.," came a voice from across the lobby. The team turned to see Deputy Park standing by the grand staircase, beckoning J.J. over.

"I'll be right back, guys," J.J. told Valentine and Trudi. "Guess I've got some unfinished business."

He walked over to the officer, who stood upright with his chest out as he approached. Standing before each other, they shared a stern, unwavering gaze.

"Deputy," said J.J.

"J.J.," said the deputy.

Park extended his hand, giving J.J. a firm handshake. "Good work on this case. You showed some real tenacity back there."

J.J. nodded curtly. "Likewise, I'll fairly admit."

"Just…never do…any of that again. For your sake as well as mine."

A smirk crossed J.J.'s face. "You know I can't promise that."

Deputy Park smiled. "I know you can't." He punched J.J. on the shoulder, walking away toward the exit of the Grande Chateau. "Keep your nose clean, kid."

Valentine and Trudi caught up with J.J. "What was that about?" asked Trudi.

"Oh nothing. Deputy Park was just super impressed by my world-class detective skills and was telling me they'd organize a parade in my honor. It'll be a low key affair, he says. Only two or three floats."

Valentine and J.J. walked Trudi back to her place at the front desk. She rounded the corner and sat at her chair, addressing them as they had first seen her several days ago.

"I guess this is it," said Valentine.

"Guess so," replied Trudi.

J.J. leaned over the counter. "And you're *sure* there's no way to convince you to roll with us? I could probably swing some equity options for you if it sweetens the deal."

"I'm sure. My place is here at the chateau. Plus, my Lola would kill me if I quit a steady job. She'd probably ship me off to a convent in Cebu."

"All right," said J.J. "Well, you can't say I didn't try. Valentine, do you think she's ready for the secret handshake?"

"I think she's ready."

J.J. looked over at Trudi. "It's actually just a big group hug."

Valentine and J.J. reached over the reception desk and embraced Trudi.

"Stay up out there," said J.J., as his brother and he began walking away.

Trudi waved goodbye to the two and watched them exit through the wide doors of the Grande Chateau. Sighing deeply, she looked down at her desk and all the work she had to do. She had her old job back thanks to her firing coming from a now-apprehended murderer. If she kept her head down and worked hard, she'd probably make shift manager in a year. A couple more years of that, maybe a transfer or two, and she'd be a hotel manager, no doubt. And with that came benefits and a livable salary, and presumably an employer-matched 401k. She could probably be a home-owner by her thirties, which for some people was a very desirable lifestyle.

Different versions of her life swirled around inside her head. She saw so many paths before her she could pursue. So many potential mistakes she could learn from.

These were very natural thoughts for an eighteen-year-old who saw their whole life before them and who also had just apprehended a cold-blooded killer after having escaped a room that was quickly filling with sand.

She got up from her desk.

* * *

J.J. AND VALENTINE WALKED AWAY from the Grande Chateau, out toward where they had parked their kickstand-less motorcycle on its side. Pockets of snow remained on the ground, but the sun was making quick work of them.

"I highly doubt we're gonna be able to get that motorcycle to start again," said J.J. "Besides, even if we did, we're out of gas. Let's see if we can hitchhike down the mountain. I'll get down on the ground and pretend they ran me over if you want to do the ride negotiations."

"Hey!" a voice from the chateau called.

J.J. turned to see Trudi de la Rosa standing in the open doorway.

"Hey," said Valentine.

She walked toward them. "Look, you two are idiots in your own right, and—"

"Hey," said J.J. "it's normal when my brother calls me an idiot, but it just feels accusatory when it's coming from you."

"I'm an idiot too," Trudi said. "My stupid deductive reasoning can only get me so far until everyone starts thinking I'm a jerk. I don't have the clue-solving skills that you have, Valentine, and I don't have the… whatever you have, J.J."

She reached them at the parking lot, searching for the words she wanted to say. "Separately, we're terrible sleuths, but if we work together, I think we can at least make one passable detective."

J.J. looked at Trudi, then over at Valentine.

They stood there for a moment. Trudi tried to think of anything she could add, but decided she had said her piece.

J.J. broke the silence. "You coming or what?"

CHAPTER 21

Epilogue

D ear Reader,
Rejoice! Rejoice! Rejoice! The prodigal son returns from ten years of globetrotting and gallivanting with the publication of the very book you hold in your hands. It is I, Dr. Cecil H.H. Mills, noted fiction scribe and author of such venerable page turners as *I Loved Infinity*, *The Spies of the Nantes Underground*, and I suppose my now-infamous magnum opus, *Cerberus, From On High*. My latest offering, *Ghost Hunters Adventure Club and the Secret of the Grande Chateau*, saw our unlikely heroes narrowly escape death to solve a surprising mystery with twists and turns alike. I hope you had as much "fun" reading it as I did writing it from an undisclosed mountain cabin that I'm renting under a pseudonym to avoid getting *Misery*'d.

I'll not mince words here, dear reader: the past few years have not been kind to yours truly. From loss, to loss, to more loss, to a protracted years-long mental breakdown, to recovery, to surprisingly another breakdown brought on via pharmaceutical experimentation through a Ukrainian holy man, to recovery again; I look down at my corporeal form and recognize that I'm ready to reenter the literary world.

Young Adult fiction was not my first choice, as I have made clear. I much prefer my weightier tomes of yore, the intellectual scrivenings that held up a mirror to the human condition and challenged what we once thought it meant to be. In any case, I've told my publishers time and again that I trust no one born after the Jonny Lee Miller/Angelina Jolie sci fi opus *Hackers* (1995) was released; however, with the threat of ham-fisted loan collectors looming over my head, I've decided to dip my toes into the frigid and sometimes unkind but usually lucrative world of flashy adventure pulp.

Nevertheless, I am here to answer your no-doubt burning questions. Have at me, dear reader, and I'll answer them with an open heart and wizened mind.

Dear Mr. Mills,

Where do you get your ideas from? I'm an aspiring writer myself and would love to get as much insight into your work process as possible.

Beatrice, age 12

Dear Beatrice,

I'll forgive you your indiscretion just once, but let this be a warning to all naysayers, bridge trolls, and uneducated simplefolk alike: it's Dr. Mills. Doctor. Doc-tor. I didn't suffer through eight years of university education and a desert-dry thesis on the motility functions of the aquatic ragworm to be called Mr. Mills, and I'll fight this in paragraphs-long diatribes until the day I die or in the event the university strips me of my title for besmirching their name, as they have several times threatened to do.

Dear Dr. Mills,

What influences your writing the most?

Elizabeth, age 14

Dear Elizabeth,

What influences me the most? What an open question. Why, it would take me years of study and volumes and volumes of belabored writing to even begin to scratch the surface of what influences me. And that's just for the academic, book-read version of your very own Dr. Cecil H.H. Mills. Decades of my life were spent wearing the hats of a street urchin, a nomadic ne'er-do-well, a riverboat scamp, a then-reformed proselytizer, and many more. I've been shanghaid, I've pitched dice with seedy boxcar-jumpers, I've won and lost fortunes by wit and by luck. All of these little bright and dark moments form a patchwork quilt of existence that bleeds from my edges and onto the page. Those, my dear reader, are my influences.

William Goldman's pretty cool, though. Definitely try and read a lot of that guy. His works really helped me figure out structure.

Dear Dr.,

I banged your mom last night.

Nathan, age 16

Nathan,

Listen here you little smeg-head. Let me ignore the low-brow and culturally devoid remark about my mother and focus instead on the intent with which I assume you wrote it. You intended to rile me up so that I may showcase my insecure underbelly built from a direct fear of nonacceptance. Allow me to assure you that most prominent writers have built a skin thicker than the skull in which your half-formed brain resides. Luckily for you, I'm not most writers. Unluckily for you, I will not forget this transgression. I will now dedicate my life and my resources to finding you, destroying you, and making you regret the day you were born on this earth. My dear Nathan, the retribution will be biblical.

And with that I have been informed by my editors that I am not allowed to openly threaten children. I would like to retract the preceding paragraph and halfheartedly apologize to Nathan and whatever late-model, dime store apparatus he keeps between his ears.

Hi Doctor Mills,

Do you have any daily rituals that help you be creative? I've tried taking cold showers recently and I've found that they make me more energized throughout the day.

Samantha, age 20

Dear Samantha,

My daily rituals will vary, especially per project and even more especially as I grow older. However, here is a close rundown of my day-to-day as I was tapping out the manuscript to this very book:

8 AM: Wake up, decide that the day doesn't deserve me yet.

9 AM: Actually wake up, take shower. Temperature of shower undisclosed.

10 AM: Breakfast at local diner. I order the usual.

11 AM: Begin writing.

12 PM: Doubt my abilities as a writer. Begin crying. Call my brother and ask him for validation. He's crying too. I ask him what about. His marriage is falling apart; he doesn't know if he can be the father to his kids that he knows he should be. We're both crying together now, trying to work through years and years of repressed guilt and regret. We know that we can make it out of this alive.

1 PM: Back to writing!

6 PM: Finish day's writing—I forgot to eat lunch again what with all the crying. I walk to the corner store and order a sandwich. Marcello's back at the counter. He looks tired. He doesn't know if the shop is gonna make it through the winter. I put a hand on his shoulder, knowing that it must have been hard for him to share this with me.

7 PM: I organize my notes for the next day, promising myself that I won't succumb to the darkness. Not today, not ever.

8 PM: Piano practice.

11 PM: Bedtime. The ghosts of my past will haunt me, yes. But we're old friends now. I greet them warmly.

Dear Dr. Mills,

My father worked at Bradford & Bradford. The colossal failure of Cerberus, From On High *and the shuttering of Bradford & Bradford went on to ruin his career in book publishing and forced myself and my family to drastically change our metropolitan lifestyle in utter disgrace—moving to rural America to farm cash crops for well-to-do, heritage-branded brunch restaurants.*

In the years since we've managed to scrape by, sure, but I know my father dwells upon his failures at every waking moment of his life, and that every day when I'm harvesting kale and Brussels sprouts for twenty-something hipsters to eat while discussing their mundane problems, I'm damning your name. There are real people who suffer because of your antics. Real lives ruined by your unscrupulous business dealings.

I hope you choke.

Justin, age 17

Dear Justin,

Against my lawyers' wishes I've decided to answer this letter. I knew Gary well. He was an honest man, more honest than either of those Bradford rats. While I continue to suffer from my own personal demons with the failed publication of Cerberus, From On High *and the subsequent warehouse fire that destroyed every known copy of the book, I will say that I am no more your father's master than you are. His fate is his alone and he must embark on his own journey to take back what life has cruelly wrested from his hands.*

Still though, I understand that my response may not sate your taste buds, which no doubt thirst for blood, so I'll offer you this: upon your eighteenth birthday, you may request my personal address from your father. It's the same one he's always had on file. I will permit you to challenge me to life or death combat, with one weapon of your choosing, unrestricted. May I warn you, however, that while my bones have brittled in these later years, my mind remains sharp and plastic. I will not be an easy foe.

I eagerly await your calling.

Hi Dr.,

What do you think about "relationshipping," or "shipping" of your characters? In fandom communities, fans will usually imagine which characters might end up in romantic relationships with one another. Arguments can sometimes be heated, especially among the more hardcore supporters, so I'm curious if you have any preferred "ships" for your characters, or if you plan on interjecting romance into your Ghost Hunters Adventure Club *novels.*

Annie, age 15

Annie,

Let me tell you this right now and have it be clear as possible so that one day you'll look back on this response to your letter and know more than you did back then:

It doesn't matter.

Moreover, nothing matters. And one day when everything turns to ash, whether around you or within you, as it has to me, as it will for everyone one day in their lives, you'll wonder why you didn't spend more time being kinder to those around you. You'll think about all of those petty arguments you had and all of those cheap cigarettes you used to smoke and about your unending, insatiable hunger to be liked, and what you did to get that validation. You'll no doubt see that your heart held cruelty, in its darkest and most vile form, metastasizing outward from your heart. "Is it too late?" you'll ask yourself. "Is it too late to wake up in the morning and change and be better and do better and let kindness and love be the grounding principles of your life?"

Maybe. I'm not the one to decide that.

Hi Dr.,

What does the "H.H." in your name stand for? I've always been curious and can't seem to find the answer anywhere.

James, age 14

James,

It stands for "How about you Hmind your own business?"

Please send all questions, comments, concerns,
and gifts of high monetary value on the secondary market to:

P.O. Box 1271
Glendale, CA 91209
c/o Dr. Cecil H.H. Mills